T0020062

Moonflower, Nightshade, All the Hours of the Day

Stories
by JD Scott

First published 2020 by &NOW Books, an
imprint of Lake Forest College Press.

Carnegie Hall
Lake Forest College
555 N. Sheridan Road
Lake Forest, IL 60045

lakeforest.edu/andnow

© 2020 JD Scott

Lake Forest College Press publishes in the broad spaces of
Chicago studies. Our imprint, &NOW Books, publishes
innovative and conceptual literature and serves as the publishing
arm of the &NOW writers' conference and organization.

ISBN: 978-1-941423-05-9

Library of Congress:

Front Cover Design by JD Scott
Drawings © Marina Micheva
Graphic Design by Emma O'Hagan

Printed in the United States

LAKE FOREST
COLLEGE
PRESS

Contents

The Teenager

Something felt unclean to the teenage boy. It was the lack of separation between days, the same jeans that carried him onward. He took a bar of Irish Spring to his mouth, scrubbed at the wine stain: a red thread between his inner and outer lips. The Florida sun rose, canvasing the previous sleepless night. All the people in their box houses were waking up in air-conditioned rooms. He inspected his teeth at different angles in the medicine cabinet mirror, catching fragments of the girl moving in the bedroom behind him.

Everyone in their neighborhood grew up Catholic, and whether they were confirmed or went absent in the presence of God, they held that essence inside. The boy lived in the current of penitence and sin. His mother owned a construction business. He didn't know exactly what his father did, but it involved the word "hotels" and no one seemed to mind that it required for him to be away for weeks at a time. His father always flew first class and talked of *stewardesses* and *monuments* whenever he returned home. The teenage boy lived unchaperoned, preferring to find guidance in his one friend. The teenage girl wore too much eyeliner and made decisions for them both. They were of the same stock. They got each other, and it was this understanding that propelled such grief between them. This existence of credit card and gated community allowed him to feel violenced as they moved back toward the inebriated day.

"Are you almost done? I need to do my hair," the girl said behind his reflection. He combed his hair using fingernails, tucking loose strands into the plastic frame of his sunglasses.

"I'm done," he said.

"I didn't do my biology homework."

"It doesn't really matter," the boy said.

* * *

The girl lived in a house covered in coquina shells—a sterile, coastline castle that her mother won in a settlement. Her father was from Cuba, owned a tile company. Her mother slept a lot. When she was awake, she moved through the house as if her body were made of syrup—ignoring her daughter's empty wine bottles, making her way to the fridge for some cold-pressed juice.

There were tiny straws scattered on the silver coffee table. The boy scooped them into his jacket pocket and thought about extinct animals, although he wasn't sure why. He was zombied and fogged by sleeplessness. The dodo was the only one he was certain of, and maybe a carrier pigeon or something that looked like a zebra. Its name was hidden in a place he could not access at the moment. He felt that if he rubbed his tongue along the roof of his mouth long enough, at least one of these elusive insights would return.

The girl tried to put her hands in the boy's pocket, and he swatted her away. She shuffled through a small black make-up bag, stained with light powders and red blotches of something. She pulled out a smaller white bag. She pulled out a ring of keys saying, "I bought it, so I can do it when I want."

Half of a metallic heart dangled from the girl's key chain. It displayed the word BEST. The boy possessed the other half, which read FRIENDS. She gave the boy this tchotchke as a sign of ownership rather than sentimentality. He kept his half in his backpack alongside Wite-Out and a half-eaten pack of Lance sandwich crackers. There was something mathematical to the girl's actions, the way everything had a purpose, the way her hands moved in the air like an invisible audience was always watching. She dipped her car key into the white bag. The crystal flakes refracted light. "Meet my good friend Bumper McKey," she said to no one. The powder disappeared. She repeated the steps—replacing her face with the boy's. He rubbed his tongue around his mouth and thought, "Vanishments. Tasmanian wolves. Somnambulisms. Nice to meet you, Bumper McKey."

"Wait here," she said, "I need to wake Mom up and get lunch money."

"Is she awake?"

"I don't know."

"Will you eat lunch?"

"I don't know," she said, walking away.

He put on lip balm and wore his sunglasses

and could taste the bitter herb dripping in the back of his throat, mixing with old tannins. He loved the directions, the instructions, the way the girl ordered him and provided movement. He felt an age that was mystic inside him, as if he had slipped through a magical doorway, found some way to circumvent existence as a high schooler. The calendar was erased; for a moment, he forgot what day it was. School though, that was a constant. Static electricity galloped in the back of his throat. To be this person was to be adult, refined. The kind of person who only drank red wine. He thought of the Virgin Mary, tried to remember her prayer in Latin, although he wasn't sure why. Thoughts came to him like this.

The girl came back into the bathroom, slipped the bag of powder into his jacket pocket saying, "If it's on me I'll finish it before we get to school," in a voice that he found untrustworthy yet agreeable.

* * *

On the interstate, there was a powerful clarity in the upper hemisphere of the boy's body. There was that thought surfacing again: the extension between one day and the other becoming severed, the breadth between virtue and hubris becoming blurred. Day, night, everything felt controllable and protected. Intense recall—those extinct zebras—they were called quaggas. He sang words in his head until they annoyed him. The music on the radio reminded him of light bulbs dropped against linoleum. He desired only one song, but did not know its title or lyrics, only a little bit of its melody. The boy felt like a chauffeur, felt like he was always driving someone around, although he didn't have a license yet.

The girl held a notebook in her lap. She wrote in print, but never picked her pen up. Everything became a cursive. She tried to miss as many classes as possible, but homework somehow felt necessary and guilt-inducing, which might have been the Catholic in her. She was the Polaris of truants. It surprised the boy again and again that she kept up the performance of trying. He saw a sign for Starbucks from an exit, thought about breakfast, remembered eating like it was a good friend who rarely visited. He thought of school, of chemistry class. He only enjoyed the lessons on titrations: the burette which resembled some part of an IV—and the pH balance—that concentration turning pink. Orange juice: acid. Whole milk: base. Coffee…acid? Maybe a base if you add milk? The girl screamed and kicked her foot into the phantom brake of the glove box, and the boy slammed his foot down until there was no more movement or noise, just a faint smell of something burnt, or burning. The boy hadn't noticed the contrast between the speeding cars and traffic halted up ahead, which was not ahead, but where the car sat at its current moment. No damage had been done, but the cars in the other lane felt personified to the boy: the headlights of the sedan behind him like giant pupil-less glare.

"I've only had this for two months and my mom would kill me if it got dented," the girl said. She was sitting with her arms crossed, an empress of leather throne. Her knuckles were white, pen gripped in her shaking hand. The boy didn't say anything. He couldn't imagine the girl's mother lucid enough to get angry, let alone kill anyone, but he kept his mouth shut.

"Let's go the other way to school," the girl said, "I hate the interstate."

He signaled and went down the off-ramp and felt relieved, calmer with the distance from that one spot, where he imagined everyone was still talking about him, the screeching tires, the asshole who didn't watch the road, and how everyone almost died, or worse, ruined a good paint job.

* * *

At lunch, the boy bought pizza from the cafeteria. The chemical cheese slid off its tomato-flesh, onto his tray in a plop, leaving a red triangle behind. He bit into the clump once before slipping the rest into a nearby trashcan. He wanted a salad, or something covered in dirt, and he wondered if that meant he needed more zinc. There were facts somewhere in his head, he knew them, where did they go? Maybe it was iron? This thing that he needed. Cravings. Geophagy? The girl called him. He picked up the phone and a woman, some teacher he had never seen before said, "No cellphones on school grounds." She repeated it with her arm extended. "You, with the cellphone. Hey, hey you there!" The boy walked into the men's bathroom and locked himself in a stall that smelled like lasagna.

"What was that about?" the girl said.

"A teacher. She was yelling about my phone."

"Tell her to fuck off. I called into the office and signed you out for a doctor's appointment."

"What kind of appointment?" he asked.

"Does it matter?"

"I want to know in case they ask."

"Fine. Ear appointment."

"Did you say 'ear appointment' when you called into the office or did you just make that up right now when we were talking? I just want to make sure."

The girl hung up.

The bell rang and he walked out into a sea of bodies. He could see the teacher somewhere behind him, standing erect, darting her eyes around, searching. He felt sorry for her, but mostly because her head reminded him of a toothpaste cap, and he thought that was no way to live.

* * *

The student garage was too small, and most of the teenagers had parked in an overspill of too-tall grass on the property. The boy stood with green brushing up past his ankles. There were still three hours left in the school day, and he didn't know how to measure them. He bent down to pick a blade that he could whistle with, but got distracted by how wet the earth beneath his feet was. It felt like a small wilderness to have his shoes leave the asphalt lot. Everything suddenly felt dirty, and he wanted to be inside the car, to cleanse himself in some way.

"Where are we going?" the boy asked.

"I don't know. Let's just drive around."

"I don't want to drive."

"Okay, I'll drive," the girl said.

She cut a nugget of weed with safety scissors whenever they stalled at a red light. The green bits fell onto an *Introduction to Wicca* book she kept in her car. The boy focused on the cover's esoteric sigils until those designs made him dizzy in his daydreams of casting spells. He turned his focus to the rapid motion of scissors slicing. The scissors' handle was pink and it reminded the boy of titrations, and he regretted something, but he couldn't find the word in his head to match the feeling.

All the buildings they passed seemed the same to him: strip mall after strip mall of Burger King, Publix, Smoothie King, Vitamin World, Steinmart. They passed a barbecue restaurant, the sweet smoke rising up from somewhere, and he wondered if the girl had dissected a pig fetus yet. They had never talked about fetuses. The teenagers parked in a K-Mart lot and smoked a pipe until the air felt thicker and crawling, pushing them out into the balmy afternoon. The boy asked if K-Mart had a popcorn machine. The girl said that's gross, and she didn't remember. The boy looked at his shoes and said he needed a new pair, and the girl replied with, "Yes, always," as if everything physical was a variable to be manipulated and obtained.

They walked between aisles of scuffed linoleum,

and the girl put things into her purse that the boy knew she didn't need. The boy found a pair of shoes like the ones he was wearing. He brought them into a dressing room and put his old shoes in the new box and the new shoes on his old feet. The whites of the rubber soles were fluorescent. He felt holy. *Et benedictus...Et benedictus....* He whistled hymns as he looked down the deserted aisles.

He found the girl, and she said she felt nervous, like someone was watching her. He said they should leave from the garden exit because it was less crowded, and who would want to steal a plant anyway? They wandered outside and walked beside bags of mulch and something that smelled like hospitals. He thought of his father dragging fertilizer on the tomato garden his mother planted when he was younger. Nothing ever sprouted, and they never tried again. The boy saw a Venus flytrap and put his finger between its soft teeth. It lazily closed its mouth. He asked the girl if she could get it for him, and she said no, and what did she just say, and she didn't want dirt spilled in her purse.

There was a tall man with a buzzed head and bodybuilder arms by the store exit. The boy remembered a movie where a hero walked through a gate of Sphinxes and they shot laser beams out of their eyes. That part frightened him as a child, and he felt frightened now as he walked between the parallel security gates. He expected the high pitch of an alarm, as if red lights would go off and spin around everywhere like a nightmarish game show. He felt relieved when nothing happened, until the tall man said, "Excuse me, you two there, excuse me."

The girl took off running in the direction of her car. The man changed his passive stance and moved toward the boy saying, "Excuse me, son, I need you to empty out your pockets." The boy ducked around the man and took off running in a different direction from the girl. Was this instinct? The tall man chose to chase him instead of the girl, long legs making strides, his tallness in the boy's periphery, behind him, grabbing onto the boy's jacket—but the boy flew out of it like a shell, a different skin. He kept running and looked back—the man had somehow tripped in the blur of motion. He was on the ground and trying to get up and the boy could hear an adrenaline voice in his own throat throbbing *yes yes yes yes yes* and he kept running around the side of the parking lot and there were trees in the back and he didn't stop and flew himself past the branches and one scratched his face and he kept running and his shoes slid through mud and a saw palmetto scratched his ankles and he tumbled over a low tree branch and hit the ground.

His face was hot, mouth gasping for air. He didn't want to be heard, so he bit his lip shut and pushed air heavily in and out of his nostrils. He tasted metal, dirt, maybe zinc. His boxed ears only heard something rising, compressing inside his body. He thought about the tall man, the girl, police. Fingerprints. Dirty fingerprints. He thought of his mother, his father, his favorite jacket, and then the little bag of blow in the pocket, and he wasn't sure which one he missed the most. Music cheeped from his jeans. Scrambling, he ripped the battery out from the back of his phone, fearing someone from the store might have heard the noise. He stood up, feigning quietness, and walked farther into the moist terrain.

Was this nature? For the first time he wondered why people settled in Florida. Who would want to live in a bog of insects and steaming air? He understood why people would want to build over it though, suffocate it by casting it into concrete. Mosquitoes buzzed and bit and he kept rubbing the back of his hand on his face. He was getting lines of blood and dirt all over himself. Some salty part of himself burned his eyes. It stung every time he blinked. The new shoes already looked like his old ones: wet, slobbering, and filthy. It's fine, he thought. He could explain this. He could get home, take an extra-long shower. This swamp beat juvie, and upon realizing that, he found some pleasure in not being caught, of going into the confession booth and just sitting quietly, smiling. Although some part of him still believed he was in trouble, and it was this fear that pushed him deeper into the landscape.

The teenager walked into a camp of sorts. There was an orange traffic cone nailed to a tree and splotches of red spray splattered against the bark of another. There was a broken folding chair and layers of blankets on the ground, sheltered only by blue tarps nailed between trees. There were crushed aluminum cans covering some magazine with a naked woman on the cover. He leaned against a tree for a long time, focusing on the sweat and the ache of his body.

After his legs grew tired and he convinced himself that no one was coming to look for him, no one was going to trigger his feet to run again, he sank to the ground. How long had this camp been here? Was it still in use? What kind of person would live here? He thought of the homeless people he saw sleeping at the foot of the Sacred Heart church downtown, and how he would have liked that better, if he were homeless. Cold stone. Concrete. No trees. Less insects. He took the shoes off and sat down at the edge of the blanket. He watched the shoes intently, as if they held some mystic gift to call out and fix everything.

* * *

The sun set into a full moon; the light was still adjusting itself—a confusion of orange and stars. The boy wondered what happened to the girl. She must have gotten away, right? Sped out of the parking lot, circling the suburbs, devising a plan to rescue him. That's what she'd do, right? How many times did she try to call? Which amount was enough? Did she tell her mother? His mother? Was anyone looking for him? What punishment was headed his way? This was an afterlife of sorts, he thought. The phrase "the moral of the story is" repeated itself inside him, but there was only white space after the verb. The trees rustled.

A man came through, carrying a piece of plywood like a staff. In the dull light the boy could see a broken bottle of beer tied to the top. He was wearing a dirty shirt with a map of Florida on it that said ASK ME ABOUT MY GRANDKIDS. His face was begrimed and his beard was frazzled—an electrocuted cartoon. The boy wasn't sure what a shaman looked like, but it sounded like the correct word for this stranger.

"Who the hell are you?" the man asked in a low growl. The boy imagined the broken glass being dragged across his neck. The late-night news and all the JonBenét Ramseys of the world made him fear something that he couldn't put a finger on until now. He said nothing.

The boy was bewildered and wanted to laugh or maybe cry, but staying completely still seemed to be the most non-threatening action.

"What, you deaf? Get the hell out! Get the hell out of my home!" the man shouted. The boy realized he was now lying on the blanket and the blanket was under the tarp and that was probably a home by some sense of the word, so he stood up and stepped to the side. The man leaned on his staff and closed his eyes, as if an intense focus was needed to summon his thoughts. The boy thought about pushing him over and running. Homeless people are probably easy to kill, he thought. Was this instinct? He thought about sharp glass, quaggas, prayers, and still he did nothing.

"Why are you here?" the man asked impatiently.

"I'm hiding," the boy replied, surprised at his

own honesty. The man laughed, but it was more like a howl, which turned into something more like a cough, and then spit.

"Good boy, good boy," the man repeated. He licked his lips and frowned. The boy stepped back a little. The man asked, "Do you think I'm going to hurt you?"

The boy asked, "Do you think I'm going to let you hurt me?"

Neither of them said anything for a long time.

"What did you do?" the man asked.

He had been so good at lies before: fictitious friends and coffee shops, a spreadsheet of alibis, touching himself under a blanket that God couldn't see through. What could he say? The powders and smoke, the pockets and purses. Guilt was genetics, it was conditioning. Silence was preferred in the company of strangers.

"What did you do?" the man asked again, approaching. Which sin to confess? Does the word "parable" only appear in religious texts? Was everything else a fable, a fairytale, a myth?

"I stole," he said, pointing down to the caked shoes near his bare feet, which throbbed with mosquito bites. It was a safe choice, a tangible sin. A little truth. The man put his hand on the boy's shoulder, finger sliding under the collar-line of his t-shirt. *Et benedictus fructus ventris tui.*

"Do you think I had a son? Do you think he looked like you?"

Was this a non-sequitur? He couldn't imagine this man with a son, a family, anything besides this tarp and traffic cone. He thought, for the first time, how someone ends up living in the undergrowth behind a strip mall. This felt like a lesson. *The moral of the story is.* Be rich. Grow up. Be white. Be tall. Be a man. Be blameless. Be that type of adult. Only fuck up when no one is watching. Or fuck up in public if you hold the power. *Who holds the power?*

"I don't know," the boy said. "You look like a shaman." Into the confessional booth of night. In all the books he read in school, the hermits were wise. The people who disappeared were wise. The evasive were wise. What story was he projecting on this stranger? The man rubbed the boy's collarbone with dry, dirty fingers. What was "sheer madness"? Why did people say that? He thought of safety scissors slicing weed. Shears. *Introduction to Wicca.* Why were some rituals privileged and others not? Only prayers held sacred. *Ora pro nobis peccatoribus.* The teen boy's mind connected in tempests. One thought, then the next, storming on. Pops of power and toxins and blood and spit. He knew why the man asked the things he asked. The man knew the boy would not have come into this camp of his own volition. Cause and effect. Biology. There, too, was a heat lightning occurring inside him and anything could happen at any second and his entirety was reduced to a stranger's fingers. Quaggas, quaggas, quaggas.

They stood there, unspeaking, connected by uncomfortable touch. The boy thought of everything he could say. Escape routes, conversational resurrections. He thought he should have empathy for this man, but he possessed so little that even the concept of understanding a stranger's pain felt as unknowable as a shaman. There was nothing but this moment when all things could get better or worse like all things do and could, and the man rubbed the boy's pulse point, worked his way to his Adam's apple, palm held steady. Anatomy. *Nunc et in hora mortis nostrae.* The boy moved his smaller, cleaner hands to his own shoulder, letting them rest there—then, over the man's fingers. First, gentle. Then he squeezed. His grip was weak, but he enclosed the man's hand with all of his strength, old bones cracking beneath his urgency to demonstrate violence. The man let go, pulled back, shaking. *Amen.*

The moon settled and nothing danced. Palmetto bugs shifted beneath the marsh grass. Broken glass sheened. They both stood there, listening for another human's voice. Cannibalisic images flashed in the teenager's head. His body splayed out, pinned to the tree like that orange cone.

Then, "Go home." That's what the man said. That was it. "Go home."

Had he gotten away with it again? The boy crouched, moved out of a distance where the shaman's fingers could reconnect. The boy reached down to pick up the shoes he had set by the blanket.

"No, the shoes stay here," the man said. "I own them now. Leave before I own you too."

How could he get home without shoes? What would his mother say? What would he say when he saw her? The only path he knew was shoes. Every day he wore shoes, and he could not leave without shoes. Even dirty shoes were shoes. This was survival. The boy grabbed onto the pair and with a quick movement the shaman prodded the boy's arm with the glass-staff. The boy didn't mean to cry out as loud as he did. He was bleeding from his forearm: that thin type of blood, paper-width, coating his skin with an odd symmetry.

He felt this pool of id inside him, wanted to sink his teeth into the man's neck and mimic the same wound. It felt animal, biblical, vampiric. He hesitated, adding up the math of blood, this thirst to destroy himself and all others. He would murder this false shaman and every homeless man who looked like him. *This is power.* The boy screamed again, no longer at the empty air, but directed toward the man. The man beckoned with two fingers and a cottonmouth smile. What is the nature of prey? What is the effect of blood hitting air, iron-stench stretched into the humid, filthy dark?

The longer the boy stood and stared, waiting for himself to move, the slower his heart shrilled for him to kill. He felt a sadness. Something not unlike pity. The rage felt as if it was flushing down his legs, moving from his bare feet into the wet earth. Why were his legs still in this spot? Why was he?

The boy turned on his bare feet, running in the direction that felt right. The man cackled, spoke to a son-figure that was no longer there. A child. An object. The voice growing mute. Body moving away from body. The boy slowed down when the parking lot glowed through the palmettos and live oaks. The lights of commerce felt familiar, safe. He walked out from the wooded area, twigs pushing up under the arch of his feet. What dimension had he descended into? It was like he fell into the spells from that book in the girl's car, entered a world outside the rules he knew how to manipulate, control.

The parking lot looked alien now. He felt the texture of concrete as he stepped back onto the edge of the lot. Although the sun had set, the ground was still emitting warmth. When did the sun set again? Was it really that late? Walking the perimeter past a giant clay pot, he noticed all the K-Mart customers were gone, the sidewalk plants moved back inside, the gate closed. Under dim security lights, he could still see Venus flytraps in the shadows between other potted plants.

Beyond the garden section, some lights were still emitting from the main store. Those who lingered inside came from another world too. They were there to put commodity on shelves. Night-shift survivalists. The parking lot was empty except for a few cars scattered. Stock boys and backseat sex. The boy wondered where the loss prevention worker went, what happened to him. Did he go home, angrily sitting in an arm chair, throwing back a beer, obsessing over that teenage boy, the one who got away? The boy who had ran into the swamp had come back, re-entering the stillness of the suburbs, where he moved around inside the same body. Almost the same. There was a new wound, but he would force it to heal.

The teenage boy walked onward. His vulnerable feet made him feel remote and untouchable. He thought of his feet in the sand at Fort De Soto Park, and his feet pushed into the St. Augustine grass of his grandparents' backyard. His feet approaching his own failed childhood garden where the tomato seeds did nothing. He thought of his feet in his old shoes and tried to not think about his feet as they were right now. Unprotected. Urban legends of needles on the ground skittering toward him.

A stale scent of French fries carried through the breeze; the McDonalds at the far corner of the plaza was the only other store left with its lights on, although it looked empty. The familiar scent of fast food maintained within him some bravery. The teenager walked to the end of the lot where the main road stretched on for miles. He wondered where the steady flow of cars was headed to, now that everything was closing, or closed. Where did these people have to be? Wasn't it late? Didn't they have families? Morning jobs? School? He was more untethered from the schedules of the world than ever before. He stepped out into the road and looked up at the traffic light, and the light down the road, and the next one: a distant firefly. All the lights were blinking in unison, a steady caution of yellow, the pulsation: on and off and on again.

He stuck his thumb into the air and felt cinematic. Is this how the girl felt, with all those invisible people watching? Where had she gone? Who had she told? Would the two of them ever be the same again? *BEST / FRIENDS*. Would he go to juvie tomorrow? Could he hide his gash, his feet? He felt like such a child. How could he get home without the girl, without corroboration, without her to tell him what the real story was? What could he say that wouldn't ruin everything? The moral of the story was.... A red car pulled over to the side of the road, first slow, then slower, and then the emergency blinkers came on. A white woman with curled gray hair rolled down her passenger window. She looked welcoming, yet suspicious.

"What are you doing out here? What happened? Do your parents know?"

All he could say was, "Some friends played a mean prank on me, and I need to get home."

This was the language he knew best, his voice sliding toward smallness. His age was quelled: he was a child and this woman was his mother and she was so sad and so sympathetic and said, "Get in, get in, I will take you home. What did they do to you? Where do you live? You poor baby, you poor, poor baby," and all he could say was, "I'm sorry. I'm so, so sorry."

She touched his shoulder after he got inside the car. Her pointer finger grazed his bare neck, goose bumps erupting from that spot where a shaman's hands had blessed him. He made sure he held his arm up at the right angle, so she saw it, saw what had happened to him in the distorted light of her sedan. He wanted a witness before he went on to change the story, to erase, to make things right again with himself situated in the spot that felt like his.

He pulled down the visor and looked at his face in the mirror. There was a scratch on each side of his face, resembling war paint. Somehow, blood had gotten between his inner and outer lip. The body's wine. Another red thread. He licked his dirty finger, covered it in saliva and started scrubbing again.

Chinchilla

My lover was gifted a chinchilla on his eighth birthday, one of those creatures that seem to exist solely for childish whim. The first time I saw Angelito I couldn't figure out if he was a hamster, a squirrel, a rabbit, all three, neither, something more, maybe lab-made. They don't look like something that could actually exist in the wild, casually eating shrub grass on the side of some mountain. They were made for the safety of cages and homes. It's hard to even see them as real, but I soon came to see Angelito exactly as he was: a living, breathing chinchilla, and an especially willful one.

He willed himself through my lover's jockish middle school years, through his teens ignited with violence, even past his early twenties, which were known for remorse. Angelito was eighteen when I met my lover. Angelito could buy porn, purchase lotto tickets, attend college. This was how our jokes went. Youthful benchmarks, how maybe he'd make it into Guinness if we bankrolled his continued rodent life long enough. Angelito had willed his existence for so long—past fad and impulse buy—and now his little life was all continuity: sitting in cage, shivering, sleeping, living, living.

We, too, were living—in the city—sharing a studio that rented for thousands. The shower had no pressure and took fifteen minutes to heat up. I could usually fry an egg up and eat it on the toilet while the water was still lukewarm. I considered this vigilance. Angelito's cage took up a good eighth of our apartment, vertical with its many tubes, wheels, water bottles, and hammocks. Ours was a minimal space, but we survived in it. No wall art. No television. Only a loveseat for lovers—no other sofas or recliners. A black glass coffee table in front of the loveseat, and Angelito on display in front of that: our only entertainment. We had a tall, thin pub table with duet chairs in one corner that I referred to as the "breakfast nook." I tried to inject some romance into this life where I could. Our city life was arduous, endless. We had no occupations, no vocations. I was a master of none and took gigs where I could find them. My lover cut coke on the black glass, placed the flakes into smaller glass vials. This process was occult to me: how many hands had it exchanged before reaching my lover in its lesser quantities? His hustle has no bearing on his character though. My lover was sweet, gentle. He remembered numbers effortlessly and kept the product in steel boxes, travel-sized, each with a unique combination. I had a book on numerology that I kept above our toilet, but I never seemed to remember what each digit represented. These were our differences, our similarities, our ciphers. In our own world amongst eight million people, we somehow always made rent, found the strength to not die, to keep on.

Of course, my greatest fear was not financial,

nor physical, or even related to my own mortality—it was always about Angelito. I dreaded when my lover was gone, because every second he was away a wheel of fortune spun, pulling me closer to a ticker marked DEATH, toward this fear of being the discoverer of Angelito's body. It should also be noted that Angelito was already known for sleeping heavily, even before he aged into geriatrics. His breathing would go slow and soft. I would often push my fingers through that dark fur and imagine I was pushing years from my own life into his body. I know that sounds odd, like a blood transfusion of lifeforce, but it made sense to me, even if I couldn't quite say why. Perhaps my fantasy was a way to absolve myself of all the wrongs I believed I'd done. I never was religious growing up, and it's not that I ever felt a need to harm myself or save others. It's just that all I could think about when I was alone with Angelito was how to create a world where he could never die.

When my lover had a birthday, Angelito had a birthday. I made Angelito a little party hat out of junk mail and floss, tied it around his sable head. My lover and I kissed and ordered expensive pizza that came with unpronounceable cuts of rare meat and imported herbs. I thought this is what it meant to be alive. I thought city life was infinite. I felt something, then.

I took a gig for some art trade show from an online listing, where I stuffed complementary magazines in tote bags and handed them to passersby throughout the day. Some of the younger gallery girls made comments about partying. It was always awkward for me to make oblique references to my lover's services. We were both perseveringly sober, and I felt my own phoniness when I tried to bring up our main livelihood. So… you all… like to… party? I repeated this in my head for hours, but never spoke. I wondered how I became this person: living in an apartment with illicit powders locked inside. It felt like there was a past life when this would not have been acceptable. Who was I before the city? Who had I become? I looked at ads in the magazine I was giving out, hoping to find more work, but instead got lost in South Beach fantasies after seeing an advertisement for a gallery in Miami. I saw myself in a red convertible, driving on sand, synthesizers softly playing in the background like the soundtrack of a movie.

The trade show paid me in off-the-books cash that I stuck inside one sock for my commute home, although I'm not sure why; this wasn't a place I had kept money before. Was I casting some invisible spell into the world, one that would make me divergent from my current self? Was I trying to change, leave some part of myself behind? On the subway ride home I felt a soreness in my upper arms, wishing to lie horizontal in our small bed and let the blood even out in the way I presume blood does.

It was when I finally got back to the apartment I came across the scene of the Pietà: my lover in the position of the Virgin Mary, the dead body of Angelito lying in his hands like the tiniest wounded Christ. I could only whisper *what happened* as the tears of my lover fell. When I said what happened no part of me did not know that Angelito had finally died of old age, but it came out automatic as statements regarding death always do. *What happened. I'm sorry. He was a good guy.*

In any case, I was wrong in my assumption of Angelito's cause of death. My lover had cut a mini brick of coke open, but got distracted by his own hunger before he could finish the redistribution of product. He came out of the kitchenette with a grilled cheese dangling out of his mouth—only to see Angelito taking a dust bath on the open package. Angelito loved his dust baths, as all chinchillas do. I spent the rest of the night brushing blow off his little corpse while my lover wailed from bed. The temper tantrum brought me back to questions of Angelito's origins. Some past moment before my lover met me. Did Angelito come from the Andes mountains? Was he born in captivity? And my lover? Eighteen mysterious years of his life intersecting with Angelito's—his deeds and exes and relationships with family—all mostly unknown to me. There were hints, yes, but it seemed like Angelito was the last calendar that could stretch out toward a time that was now gone forever. I don't know who my lover was before he met me. He never talked about growing up outside the city. How many siblings did he have again? What were his parents' names? What did they do for a living? Perhaps I didn't even know my lover at all—I had tricked myself into thinking that sharing a few favorite movies was enough. Good sex. Apportioning the chores. Our two or three mutual friends we went to dinner with once a month. Suddenly our love became so horrifyingly flat, defined by each other's presence: body sharing a room with body. How had I not seen us for who we actually were? I tried to imagine my own childhood intersecting with his. Playing together at recess. Sharing carrot sticks. Something innocent. These fantasies took me far from the room where I was scraping cocaine from a dead rodent's fur with a Metrocard.

Although my lover's chinchilla died doing what he loved—living—there was a selfish remorse for myself, alone. That sixth sense when you know your love is over, and it smashes into you with its ghosts. Because we lived in the city, there were few plots of land with the soft earth one needs for burial. We assumed there were fines for touching grass since there was such a dearth of it. You couldn't even smoke a cigarette outside anymore without someone throwing a court order your way.

There was an old church nearby that had freshly laid sod, and we came in the middle of the night, Angelito's body wrapped in a cloth patterned with blonde-curled baby angels. It wasn't the reverse-grave-robbing that was unusual, but more-so the fact it was a warm summer night and no one was around to witness our peculiar ritual in an otherwise crowded part of the city. I tied off the patterned fabric with a silk ribbon. They were both bought in the Garment District. I had made a special trip, browsed for hours. I thought my lover would find this attention to detail sweet, but the cute body bag went unacknowledged. The goodbyes were quiet, and there, too, is where we buried the last of us.

On a day-to-day basis I would mostly categorize myself as "unhappy." Occasionally a song will stir some gooseflesh out of my skin, or a sad movie will feel like it's pulling apart the oyster shell that surrounds and protects the raw meat I call my heart. I didn't feel much. This is to say: I didn't have much to spare. My lover was immediately gone in our small, shared space. It was minute: an extra inch suddenly between us in bed. At least, these were my own measurements of the ephemeral. I tried to pull, to latch on, but it was of no use. Nothing I said was enough. The gap increased between us. I tried to enter past his skin with my touch and confirm some bond between us, but each caress was slightly lesser. And then I felt it too—this distance—although there was still allegiance, it was transforming. I finally knew what it meant to love someone, but not be in love with someone. They say this in the movies, but it was a concept unknown to me.

I'd like to think of myself as simple, someone whose revelations aren't as revealing as they should be. I suspect I may be dumber and less trusting than I tell myself, which seems like an adverse combination. Before I was sober, there was a brief period where I wasn't. Before I put everything in my body, there was a period where I had never put anything in my body. I had a theory that people couldn't actually get high and everyone was just pretending; it was a monumental inside joke. Some type of Saint

Vitus' Dance: massive bodies of people acting out. Anyway, I guess I just don't believe something is real until I experience myself. I don't think either of us consciously knew that Angelito was the glue that bound us as lovers, although perhaps something deep inside me wondered. There were a lot of thoughts I repressed. I told myself the city is a place where you do anything to survive. That you have to keep going for the city. That I had to keep going for my lover, for Angelito—but Angelito was dead. This love, also, dead. And my zeal for the city…. Is it possible for an epiphany to unmanifest?

When it came time for our lease to be renewed, we went our separate ways. Our love had become something unrecognizable to us both. He moved out a month before me. He took everything with him except that colossal cage. For those final thirty days I slept in a sleeping bag on the floor. We had built a wheel for Angelito together that we called the *chin spin*. In my half-sleep, I kept thinking I heard it spinning in the middle of the night. I dragged the cage to the curb after that. It took three or four trips to get it downstairs. I marveled at the emptiness it left behind. Even in this epilogue, I still heard metal squeaking one or two times in the middle of the night before I moved out. Perhaps like this Angelito had become part of me.

My lover and I never talked after that. Something in me—that dedication to survival— of being in a place without much grass or trees— that too departed with the lease. I had to get out of the city. It was no secret that I grew up in the suburbs, but I had unlearned it. I never mentioned it. Downplaying your metropolitan ways could be seen as a sign of weakness in the city. I had no goals, few skills, and could not afford to be seen as weak. I had become some sort of modern hunter-gatherer, where I could only buy the groceries that I could carry home. I was stronger than people gave me credit for. I used my time well. I resisted the limited hours of the day, trying to squeeze a few more in, running an extra errand here and there. Even buying something as simple as a screwdriver became an activity I had to artfully plan my entire week around.

That was my existence for so long. I didn't know how to re-adjust to this other life where you could just get into a car and go wherever you wanted. My life was reliant on delayed trains and chamomile tea before I had no option but leave it all behind. I sold all of my possessions. I returned the keys. I left. My exodus was something more like poking a hole in one of those foil-coated balloons that don't pop as much as sadly deflate. The air—parts of my being—escaping slowly. Then, gone.

At first it was the number of trees that gave such a violence to my eyes. I counted involuntarily. This thing that happened was a remembering of the scale of America. The off-white walls of the rented condo apologizing for their own flaccidity. Half the rent, double the size. I burned sage I bought off of Amazon. I bought a junker on the internet for a couple of hundred dollars. It was no red convertible. It was held together with chewing gum. I took up smoking for the first time in years, what with the cheap cigarettes and everything, and smoked three in a row with the windows rolled up, the hot air blasting my face. Everything reeked in the equity of burnt plastic. I went through fast food drive-thrus for the novelty of it. I was amazed how I could fill a shopping cart up to its metal edge, dump the groceries into my trunk, drive that carload home. It was incredible how much food a person could purchase with access to shopping carts and cars! Although I was sad, these forgotten pleasures gave an extra cadence to my beat. I even found joy in the rotted vegetables. I did what I did because I could. I went to a furniture superstore and walked five minutes through the orange-stickered showroom before even seeing another human. Such open space brought a sense of danger upon me! It had been so long since I had encountered anything like this—a place of no people—that it had become unreal, something else entirely. I wanted to talk to someone about what it was like to leave a claustrophobic city, but all my friends were still in the claustrophobic city, so I continued to spill French fries in my lap and displace my loneliness.

I started waking up at dawn, going to estate sales. I'd buy up the belongings of the dead, flip them on online auction sites, or else other antique stores around town. It was another gig, another small stretch toward forever. No plans, no future. Only paying rent, keeping on. I'd make enough to continue, make enough to eat another greasy burger, considering the other side of whatever I had come out of. There was a wrongness to reselling dead people's belongings, even if they didn't need them anymore, but it felt better than the previous life. I felt some type of moral high ground within me, having found a task I could repeat. Perhaps this hustle could become a permanent job, a forever.

I told myself I wouldn't text my lover until he texted me first, but he never did, and I never did. I wonder if he knew he was in this quiet stand-off with me. I wondered if he missed me—or Angelito— at all. One day I was with him in the city with his sad pet, and then I was hundreds of miles away wearing sweatpants and pretending to be suburban. The truth is: sometimes there are endings and they occur so unapologetically that no sense can be made of them. You're bound by your love in a tiny box and then you emerge from the shroud, unaccompanied, walking through the presence of so much open space. I slept alone with some interior of mine sealed in a rodent's bones hundreds of miles away. I started having new dreams about cages, dreams of hundred-floored apartment complexes, dreams of shopping malls that continued into each other, endless. The further you walked into a department store, the more you entered an afterlife you couldn't return from.

The autumnal equinox had passed, and all I could think of were craft stores. Craft stores filled with cinnamon-scented brooms. Dark ribbons. Glitter-crusted plastic pumpkins. All these props felt like an ushering in of the season. The compartmental commodity of the suburbs felt real. Everything before was illusion. Years baked at brutal summer subway stations, top-floor walk-ups. But here was a world of air-conditioning and bite-sized candy. The express train from Halloween to the new year. This felt like the good death, the change I needed. I became obsessed with these ideas—about how healing capitalism could be for the soul—the safety of familiar chain stores.

I decided to park at one end of a large, outdoor strip mall. I dedicated myself to entering every store, from west to east, and speaking to someone in each one. Clothing closeouts. Nail salons. I did just that. I hello'd; I scoured the sales racks. The final store was a big box craft outlet. I nearly cried from bearing witness to those teeming aisles: the yarn, the build-your-own-doll parts, and all the Pantone hues of oil. It was junior high, I believe, when I shoplifted last. I couldn't help myself. No one was around, so I shoved a few small tubes of lemon, ultramarine, and cadmium into my jeans. The thought of those primary colors touching my thighs brought bumps to my arms. Happiness. I bought fake flowers and was so giddy at the check-out counter that I dropped my credit card twice.

When I exited the store, I had an experience that moved my body. It's this feeling I get sometimes, like if I'm caught red-handed or a celebrity I love dies. Some psychic variation of getting the wind knocked out of me. It feels like I'm panning in and out of my body, like my mind was microwaved and suddenly I'm astral-projecting. If I were religious, I'd speak in tongues. I feel hot and fucked up and lose myself in the moment. I lost myself then. The craft store, it turns out, was the penultimate shop. A tiny unit—barely any glass windows at all—stood at the end of the plaza I journeyed through: a pet store.

I made a bee-line past the fetid ferrets, beyond hamster-as-legion, into the back corner where three chinchillas sat in a cage. Black, grey, white. I wanted someone to approach me with indignation, to tell me *many people think they want a chinchilla, but most people don't know how to take care of one. Do you even know about the dust baths?* "I know about the dust baths," I'd scream. I wanted someone to fight me—maybe even physically. I would grab a pimply teenager and pull both ears until they screamed. I see that fur, and I'm uncontrollable. I loved him. I loved him wholly. I loved his impossibly dark hair, his relaxed demeanor, his softness—that rare quality that could occasionally penetrate my own misery. My own stupidity for falling for such a disposition. When he left, I lost him forever. These are the things that people say. Does allowing myself this humanness lessen me? I wonder, too, if your only experience living in the suburbs is your teen years—then you return—is your only default setting hormones and angst? Or have I been hiding away some aspect of my feelings, my hurt, because I told myself this is what I needed to go on? When you cut the years like a tarot deck, divide the past into numerologies from the book above the toilet, does one's behavior finally make sense? There was a melodramatic emergency to how much I suddenly needed him. I couldn't stop myself. How I wished the fiendishness away. How I wished life was. This desperation.... Angelito was twenty. He could have almost bought alcohol. Probably even collected Social Security if we're factoring chinchilla years into this. I'm not sure why everything has to be human years first, but it does. These stupid jokes, again, like costume pearls hitting linoleum.

I decided, in an instant, to adopt the white one, call him Diablito—an inversion of a past life. I could be this person that inhabited space. I could be like anyone. I could get a better job, take out a loan, pay mortgage on a house. A house! A perfect fit for my budding antique dealer career! Like this I felt bumps rolling up and down my arms. This new chinchilla could live into *my* Social-Security-collection years. That thought alone brought palpitations. Was this joy, the comfort of a new life beginning? I wanted something small and romantic that I could bring into this world, some euphoria that could be for me alone.

I know, from a distance, I would resemble that mania that anyone could get in a pet store. I could see, from another perspective, how this might look like an impulse buy. I'd spent too many years with his predecessor though. I earned this mania. I know about chinchillas. I know what it's like to age and find that each passing year gives you nothing, nothing, nothing. I have something, though. I have Diablito.

I have this theory that if Angelito hadn't rolled around in the coke he would have just kept on living without end. There's no scientific principle to prove this theory, but I have a hunch it will check out. Yes, I believe in numbers. Crystals and stars. UFOs. I've read about cats in Japan that grow an extra tail and age into wild infinity. I have books that say there are deeper meanings to this world; all you have to do is practice consciousness. I'm conscious.

Diablito is snowy. Little onyx craft beads for eyes. Like this he, too, seems unreal. Plush, dollish. I am dedicated, this time, to pushing my fingers into delicate down, to transferring years of my own life into this creature so refined and so soft. If I get quite good, perhaps I can leech out the chi of others, point them all like a laser beam into my little love. I've heard stories of emotional vampires sucking energy from everyone around them. I will be lightning rod, and all the world's lifeforce will pulse into Diablito, ensure that one thing in my company will last enduringly. This one is for keeps. I imagine it like this: some perpetual flux of auras pushing toward this little chinchilla, adding year after year to his lifespan. The combined effort of all Earthians!

Hundreds of years from now, when alien invaders come to our deserted planet, Diablito will still be here, sleeping on his hammock. All humans will have uploaded their energy, their lifespans, into his little chinchilla body. They will see this beautiful creature and know we were a prudent terrestrial race. They will see the happiness that humans brought into this world—the sacrifice—how they gave up everything for him. They will nod their alien heads and know this chinchilla love was everything whole and true and good.

The Hand That Sews

In our house there is a small room hidden behind a bookshelf: it was an add-on, a novelty we inherited from the previous owners. He was a librarian and she was a seamstress. She craved a space of her own, and so he built the hidden passage so she would have a place to sew. At least, that is what our real estate agent told us: the house was already empty when we put our bid in. I was pregnant with my son at the time. My husband had hurt his back playing tennis—I remember I unloaded more boxes than he did, and it was June, the house, warm.

We loved that old Tudor like we loved each other, like we loved its backstory: buy the home where a woman serged for the neighborhood. Homemade Halloween costumes! Hemlines! Clientele moving through the false panel to pick up their fitted jeans! And her dearest, a bookish husband who represented knowledge above all else!

There was a fake book in a real bookshelf, that when tugged, unlatched the hidden doorway behind the shelf. We removed it, replacing it with a simple latch. Perhaps we erased some of the charm by making the shelf-door conspicuous, but it's not like I'm opposed to wonder. I can imagine what the original owners felt: pull the spine and the door unlatches; a whole shelf of weighted words feeling airy, swinging out on invisible hinges into a different world. I understood this appeal, the enchantment of a husband and wife in love, what it means to give a gift to your only. The happy couple. Their quaint occupations. It's a good, marketable tale. It's the same reason realtors bake cookies, or apple pies, leave them out during an open house. Ours did—but it was the hidden sewing room that sealed the deal.

I came to look past the intrigue, using that space for boxes: Christmas decorations, downgraded possessions we upgraded from, unwanted baubles for the yard-sale-to-never-come. This was my calculation: for that desirable room to never hold any desire. I did not make the room off-limits; that would have only provoked interest for defiant children, and a hidden room by its nature holds mystery. I gave it the energy that it just was, and why bother wasting time among so much dust and junk? There was some hiding-and-seeking when my son and his friends were small, but that was many years ago. My son spends more time at mall arcades and bowling alleys. My husband has his home office. That room—its fascination—is still mine.

* * *

In that room there are boxes, and behind those walls of cardboard there is one closet against the back wall. This closet is filled with moth-gnawed cloth, leather jackets in plastic dry-cleaner bags. Green yarn. Knitting needles. Bowling bags. The dimensions of this closet only hold past dealings.

In that closet, if you walk in, turn around, and look up, there is a space above the interior closet door. It is flush, unnoticeable in the lightless vault of hodge-podge. My husband does not even know. For me, it requires a step-stool. If you push hard enough on the space where the panel is, it pops out like the chocolate behind an advent calendar.

In that space behind the false panel there is a safe. The combination has nothing to do with weddings, is not a birthday, a deathday, a graduation, anything to do with cats or dogs, a forgotten phone number, old address, corporate identification, license plate, social security digit, or bible verse. The safe has a number and that number is the day when I first opened the safe and put an object in and closed it again.

* * *

Ours is an equitable space. I work from home. My husband and I alternate our cooking and cleaning responsibilities, pulling our son into the day-to-day labor when we can. I admit, I have a soft spot for my only child, allowing him to slack on dishes and laundry. We still do family dinners. Our ritualistic dinners are mostly quiet. Although my son, like his friends, has his own room that he is always hiding inside: the secret portal of his phone that he descends into between forkfuls of green beans. He's not allowed to have it on the table, so he types beneath it with thumbs clacking away. The smirks at the screen, his automatic mouth answering *uh-huh* to whatever request or question comes from we who call ourselves adults. *Ricky*, I'll say. *How was school?*, I'll ask. *Uh-huh, ok, yeah, ok, haha.* Okay.

* * *

I remember my son, three years old, talking to a lamp in the corner of our hidden storage chamber. He was already tall enough to learn the trick, pull the latch, come inside. Our elderly dog had chewed the lamp's cord, and it was beyond frayed. Unsalvageable. When I said, *Ricky, who are you talking to? That's only a lamp, Sweetie*, he responded, *He looked lonely*. It was an old lamp with a pale ceramic body and black Japanese brushstrokes glazing the surface. If you looked closely, those abstract marks looked like the face of a sad, hoary man. Pareidolia. My sweet son.

Compared to his cousins and peers his age, Ricky had a prolonged sense of magic. He would touch the front door of the oven, thinking that alone could turn it on. He would point at the television from the couch, assuming it could be lit up by the hand alone. Everything was magic before he learned it was science. For a while my husband was worried—then it was so sudden—the rationalization, the obsession with facts. Ricky was consumed by dinosaurs, geodes, why the water comes from the sky, why our skin feels warm in the presence of the sun. Before we knew it, he was fourteen and starting the fast-track at a magnet school for science and technology. Eventually, he even re-wired the cord for the broken lamp so it was no longer broken. It certainly looked less lonely with its light back on.

It is good for my son to do the things that he does. He is still a sweet boy: differently curious, sharp. He wants to be an engineer. My husband, too, is sharp. He wants to retire—says we can renew our wedding vows, then. Go to an island. He says when Ricky goes off to college, it will be like before, as if our son's graduation is a time machine that could de-age us, uncallous the years. As if we could redistribute the love we took away from each other to pour into our child. And what about myself, my own keen wants, in this house with this boy, this man? I love them more than anything. They've both been sharpened into humans who make my heart swell, who take my eyes to that place, not quite teary-eyed, but glossed with a pride I resist—yet nevertheless—succumb to. What do I want? It's hard to say. At any moment, I could have anything I desire.

* * *

When my son was four, he asked me to read the same fairy tale again and again. It was about a devil who approached a man, telling him if he didn't bathe or clip his nails for seven years, he would be given all the world's wealth. The devil gave the man a green coat and disappeared. The man became so revolting in his uncleanliness that the daughters of the village would scream at his sight. They chased him away. He lived alone in a cave for the remainder. When the seven years were up, the devil bathed and groomed the man. He became the most handsome! The green coat had limitless pockets that always produced a golden coin whenever his hand entered. Instead of one, he married two daughters from the village he was chased away from. The dapper stranger! Unfortunately, when the two daughters realized his previous identity as that begrimed, blade-nailed man, they killed themselves in self-disgust. The devil came a'knocking and told the man he got two souls for the price of one. The man still had that green coat, though. This act is defined as a bargain because both parties gain something, although is it ever quite equal? And what about the two daughters? Where was their agency inside this bargain?

It bothered me that my son adored that story so much, but mostly because it led to a protest where Ricky marched around the house shouting *No bath! No bath!* He believed there was a prize for this.

* * *

A long time ago (…) I promised myself I would never get married, never have children, never own a dog (…) I never wanted to be selfless, but some chemicals and organs inside me betrayed (…)

* * *

* * *

To have a teenage son is to never hear "I love you."

* * *

My coat is not green and it is not a coat, and I promised I would never wear it, although it cannot be worn. My boy is too into his methodologies to understand why I did what I did. I made a deal so I could do whatever I wanted—only once—and within limits. I did it before he was born. I did it when children were never a variable. I did it because I saw a future in which I needed control. I did it because you can't rely on anyone else but yourself, especially not men.

The weight of being able to alter the universe's workings a single time burns worry lines in places where none should be. I look older than I should. I concern myself with creams, phials, vanities. There's been times I've considered opening the hidden safe, retrieving that fixer-of-worlds. It's almost enough: lost airplanes on the news. Police in other cities brutalizing youth. My face hot, screaming at the TV screen. All the injustices! I saw a neighbor's Labrador get hit by a car in the street out front. Not just hit, I heard the sound of its skull being crushed by two tons of tire and metal. That same day, late at night, after a work outing, I saw a car pull the wrong way up the interstate onramp. It reminds me of old math problems from my youth. Two cars traveling at the same speed, smashing into each other into cartoon flatness. There were no survivors.

I could undo it all. I could repair the grief of all of those who were affected, but I won't. In all of these scenarios everyone else is a stranger. There is no closeness. It would be a waste to betray the human necessity of self-interest.

* * *

Even in the hypothetical situation that someone found intrigue in the secret passageway behind the bookcase, didn't become bored with the old plastic pine trees, didn't turn away from dust-coated sumi-e paintings which line the floor against the wall, or find disinterest in unfashionable Northern attire in the closet...

...if they managed to find the hidden panel above...

...if they took the time to drill a hole in, to click, or to dust for fingerprints, or to enter every digit one by one until...

* * *

It is a small safe, but the scroll inside it is smaller. Only a few inches of a thick, yellowed paper, or perhaps it's the hide of some long-dead creature. Extinct. There's no words visible on the page. It almost looks silly, like a prop from a dollhouse. If you were to take a quill to the page, the liquid would not stick. The scroll has already been marked by an invisible blood-ink that nothing can write over. Nothing can replace the words bound there.

* * *

When I get the text message I move in procedure. I am sitting at the kitchen table, and then I am not. There is the brain continuously pre-planning, always considering how to move in crisis, and then there is the body being automated, willed by its own reactions and need to survive. I think of the other children; then I don't. I think of calling my husband, but I don't. There is only the flat, flat earth being leveled into mothers and sons, into Ricky and I.

I drag the step-stool against the floor with one hand while the other moves as divining rod—to the false book—and then the hurried feet, into the dim room, kicking past boxes, stumbling, opening the closet, unlatching, climbing, pushing, popping, turning, the wrist gyring dial to its limit, the learned bone movement as if turned thousands of times before, and the dull scroll in the dark space in the unwanted nook of the house, pulled down, reacting to my fingers.

No words need to be spoken. I think of my want for my son's life. I think of hurricanes, tornados, great tsunamis. Automatic associations of disaster. A volcano moving slowly down into a village. Cinematic. I think of bullets. I think of bullets again. Their shapes and smooth surfaces and how cold metal can feel to the fingertips. Fire. Hot fire. Warm. Blood. Inscriptions. A caldera full of blood. I would ask the earth to swallow entire cities whole if only my son was spared. It's something I feel deep in my chest, moving back toward my shoulder blades. A soreness, a pain, an incurable want. By this will alone the scroll begins to catch a slow flame and smoke, unknown alphabets appearing on its surface.

* * *

My desire is absolute. I have certainty, and it is willed. I collapse on the floor and the carpet is in earthquake, the cardboard is shifting away from the center of the room in a rumble. The carpet bends its molecules outside of reason. Wool and synthetic fiber become liquid, become gelatin, and what I hear are screams in a soft space: a portal opening to the one person I need. There is something diminutive to the punctuation of gunfire, that ruination in a light, airy pop. I am crying, and I am shouting *Ricky! Ricky! Ricky! Ricky! Ricky! Ricky! Ricky!* and my hands have gone into a cold space beneath the old shag, my ear half-submerged in that marmalade of strange matter. My body is locked into the humid room and my fingers stretch elsewhere, feeling the air-conditioned cafeteria past that spatial pectin. I say his name a final time and launch my arms in a grab. His waist, still small, still babied, my baby, soft stomach, all folded into the napkin ring of my arms. I pull.

* * *

Technology and engineering. Science and math. A word problem goes:

A) Is it better to be the mother without the son
     or
B) the son without the mother?

Another problem goes:

A) Is Ricky a man?
     or
B) Is Ricky my son?

They're not very complicated word problems, but I calculate them again and again all the same.

* * *

My hands run up and down Ricky's body, lifting his black pant leg, sleeve, the bottom of his black shirt, checking for anything wet and red. My son, unharmed in body, but the wide mouth opens in a pant—he's not unscathed. Whatever Ricky just witnessed, his mind is still in that place, far from the dark center of this room we crouch in. His wide mouth gasps, his upper teeth bared like he's about to cry, and then he cries. Even though he is a foot taller than me, he has collapsed in my lap, teary, mumbling, confused—wanting to be comforted by some order known to him. There is no order. He was across town, and now he is home. I have seen this pose before in religious paintings: the son who has been spread into an exhausted length. I tell Ricky his mother was given a wish, and she chose to use it on him. It is not quite true, but he nods. I don't know if he believes me, but he has no option but to believe me. The house is groaning, is re-writing its history. Ricky stares toward the scattered cardboard boxes of the dim room. He continues to nod even after I've stopped talking. He age is quelled, gone from seventeen and more like lamp-conversant than any college-bound engineer.

I think how stupid it was for the husband to be proud that he built his wife a room—how foolish it was for the seamstress to want a hidden passageway, for anyone to think the marvels of the world are given out for free. I think of all the fairy tales dedicated to tailors and cannot recall any about seamstresses. I think of the fairy tale mothers, forgotten, or else, dead, or else, evil. These roles delegated to women. Why did the two daughters kill themselves in that story? They should have abandoned the handsome stranger, ran off with each other instead. These definitions. My son not a man, but a door. That stupid librarian story again—the realtor's voice in my head—the smell of chocolate chip cookies. The smell of the selling point. The good-hearted men like my husband, whom we tolerate. I think of the mothers of the dead children. All the preciousness of mothers, falsified and constructed. I had Ricky because I had Ricky, and I came to love him more than anything. There was never a plan, never a desire for a child.

I brush his hair automatically, uncertain how both of us arrived to this intersection of our lives, this space in the room. I was wild. I used to value myself before all others. Ask a young gum-popping me about transaction; ask me what my answer would have been. I would have chosen myself first every time. The foolishness of flattening mothers, presuming sameness. I think of all the dumbness and alchemy of being a mother—when did that word become branded not only on my skin, but beneath it? The terms again. The word *mother* in semantic satiation, how what does that even mean? *Other, smother*, those six letters, M-O-T-H-E-R, the burnt hide of the scroll—its enchanted mark that gave me what I wanted—power—this space between murk and wonder.

* * *

You never went to school today.

> *ok*

You stayed home with a fever.

> *ok*

No one else saw you, no one else spoke to you, but me, your mother.

> *ok*

I went out to get you green Gatorade. You used to argue and tell me it was yellow, not green. You perceived the world so differently.

> *ok*

I left to get you Gatorade. I left on a mother's errand. I took care of my boy. He was a sweet boy, and he was sick.

> *ok*

* * *

Our words enter the air as MMS. Simple, spoken messages. I have become that mother too. The one who leaves leftovers in the fridge. The one who loves her child. the one *who would do anything for him*. My stomach sours. The walls continue to vibrate. The world is becoming something else: smoke rising from a foul-smelling paper until there is no more paper at all. There is a knock from somewhere.

* * *

I talk to Ricky, but he doesn't respond. I feel his forehead, and it is warmer than warm. I take him by his hand, and lead him out of that space. I recall a toddler-him, walking behind me as shadow; the way I held his hands like this, guided his feet which hadn't quite learned to walk yet. He was a late bloomer. He always fell. We pass the kitchen, my phone blinking in fiendish light: seventeen missed calls, emergency, emergency. There is a knock at the side door inside our kitchen. We turn up the back stairs and Ricky lingers behind me, his hands in front, mine in back, me dragging him forward, animating his bones. His steps are slow and heavy, sick in their choreography.

I never understood this role, but maybe I knew it all along. A son surges to become nothing like his parents. A father becomes a chemist and works at a healthy distance. A mother lives her life before being a mother, then becomes defined by others via this pea-sized core stuck in her meat. It is stupid how much my body will give, how out-of-my-control this linger inside me is for this sweaty face and this blood and this springy hair the texture of my own. A knock behind me, continuing, a knock, louder and more threatening—yet—waiting. The knocking of unfinished business is always patient in its hurry.

* * *

Beyond the loud rapping downstairs, the house is still. I tuck Ricky in beneath his green duvet. He curls as fetus, turning away from me, but for a moment, I half-climb in with him, pull him back. I want him to be this age. I want him to be this age where he will understand what I have done, why I have done it. We touch. His body is radiating: face mostly asleep, exhausted, muddled by a house that operates under new rules. An oven that turns on by touch, a television that lights up by will alone.

Mom, he says.
Shh, I say.
I'm sorry, he says.
You didn't do anything, I say.
Really, he says.
Sleep, I say.
Okay, he says.

I wonder what would have happened if I made it so I never was, or that I died giving birth to him, saved him some expense of a mother who goes out to run errands and never returns. Maybe I could have created a world where Ricky was never born, but how can I imagine a life different from the one I've lived? Should I have waited? That scroll. My indecisiveness, my desires, my heart—they all ruin me. None of this matters. The time for questions—for world movements—is over. I turn Ricky toward me once more and give a peck on the lips, thick as my own. The wallpaper, the elderly lamp. The two trophies on the top of the bookshelf. Little victories. Pushpins pinning band posters to the back of his bedroom door—all these ordinary objects I touch as I make my way out of his room.

* * *

Even from upstairs the knock does not diminish. The hand that knocks is the hand that shapes; it is also the hand that soaks blank wool in yellow dye again and again until it becomes an uncanny green. It is the hand that attaches gilded buttons, and it, too, is the hand that provides.

Sorry, Ricky says, a reply to a statement no one made. I close the door behind me, turn, begin my descent to entertain that guest, who fastens coats with a gift-giving hand, who sews for one mother after another mother after another and another and another. I focus on my body, its own radiating warmth, the smooth texture of the bannister, and my arms visited by that room where my hands slipped into a cold cafeteria across town. Although only my arms entered that place, I imagine all the blood as I move down the steps. All of my blood. And the other mothers' children hiding under tables and in bathroom stalls with their feet lifted up on the toilet seat. In the cafeteria kitchen's meat locker. Beneath the wooden bleachers of the gymnasium. Like that old sewing room: the purpose is to be unseen, to not be found.

My phone rings again. Husbands. Other mothers. The police. Wishes to rewrite their own worlds in ink. Beyond the stained glass of our kitchen-side door, there is a form, darkened beyond green panes. I can see the shadow of a hand knocking and knocking. Its rap in rhythm to the voices that once filled this house. *Ok. Sorry. Haha. Uh-huh.* When I touch the doorknob, I close my eyes, as if to heighten the ears, to parse all the sounds that separate this world from the next. The ringing. The cold, plastic thud of ice falling inside our freezer. A songbird, somewhere, sings too. Wood creaking beneath me as I shift my weight contrapposto. All of this music.

On the other side of the stained glass, a woman's hum moves into the ambient sound, not unlike a lullaby. It's a song I remember, a song that left an impress on that old scroll. I go to speak, but what could I say? The humming stops. Maybe some request I couldn't even put into the front of my mind was heard. A haggle; a negotiation; an amendment to a pact. Maybe she will forgive me this humanity, give me back to my son. If anyone would understand, it would be her. I open the door.

In the distance: the barely audible sound of an ambulance wails like some old, electric ghost.

Cross

It's Tuesday. Into the gym I go: strength-building, weight-training, core-defining. It is not the type of body that generally gym-goes, but I go, and I go gorgeous. I go to a potluck after. I am swole and famished; I carb-fill. Pizza with olives on top. Cheese-coated breadsticks dipped in liquid garlic. *Who brought pizza to a potluck?* someone asks. *I wish spring would make up its mind,* someone else says. Other people announce similar thoughts. The voices continue on in the divinity of casual conversation. *Can you watch my cat for a week?* I ask someone. *Can you watch my cat for a week?* I ask someone else. *Why?* they ask. *It's almost Easter and thus I have to be crucified,* I say.

Because I am at Pontius Pilates, that means it is Wednesday. It is the morning. My body is alphabetical—T, X, Y, a really screwed up K that pushes me to my limits. I am on the foam mat and my legs bend into the air. I am off the foam mat and my arms bend into the unknown. All these letters I have become.

Can I suspend my membership for a week? I ask. *Probably not,* the membership coordinator responds. *It's for religious reasons,* I say. *I am being crucified,* I say. *In that case,* the membership coordinator says, *I can make an exception. Pilates are good practice for being nailed to a cross*, the membership coordinator says, as if I do not know this already.

I eat a lot of homemade bread, guttered down with wine. My cat is named Judas. My father was a carpenter. I understand how all of this might sound. I am lesser. I dabble in whittling. Spoons, cartoon figurines, whistles, clothespins with outlandish alligator jaws. My largest project has been an axe. The metal was an old rust-piece found at an antique mall. Since then it has been de-aged, un-rusted, anachronistic as the old head found its way onto a freshly carved body. I have shared many photos of my handiwork on the currents of the internet. My axe has been featured on many prominent handcraft lumberjack blogs.

Later, when the city has gone to bed, I go to Papa John's website and order my favorite—anchovy and olives. I slide the time-frame button that says *ASAP to next week*. In the comments section I leave a note for the pizza artist: *All these days in–between is not an accident! I am leaving town for Eden! I am being crucified and I will not be back until then! Please do not deliver ASAP!*

At dawn it is another Wednesday, and I begin to pack my backpack (clothes, silver wristwatch, smartphone, toothpaste, Chapstick, hemp rope, my axe...). This is where the movements change— how the muscled body becomes prepared to trek at length—the back already feeling the phantom of all the weight it will suffer. I prepare to be scourged. I walk east.

The walk can be condensed into: windmills and hay devils, red farms, dead crops, cows, horses, cows, cows, highway rumble strips, purple weeds, heliotropes, semis, vultures, crows, cars. Sea grapes, saw palmettos, sand. I walk across the Atlantic. I walk through the Strait of Gibraltar; Tangier and Tarifa; Ceuta cornered as I expand into the Alboran Sea. I sit on the waves and comb my hair, brush my teeth in the brine. Catania past the toes of Italy. Tunisia. In Beirut I land. I take a selfie with the water behind me. I send it to my friend who is caring for my cat. A picture of my cat comes back, ground chicken on whiskers. Judas looks happy, although can a cat's face ever show its true interior?

When I arrive at Eden it is still Wednesday, the sun still high in the sky. The well-watered garden has vines climbing down and gnarled roots rising up out of the earth, and it's impossible to get in unless you know someone or are a good talker. After that whole serpent incident, security became tighter. I know this sounds ridiculous, but that's just how things are when you're supposed to be crucified: everything, by its essence, becomes slightly over-the-top.

At the entrance to Eden there is a giant plastic egg with a digital screen hovering in front of the gate. High noon: the shadow under the hovering egg is a small circle. The screen lights up as I approach. *Security*. On the toy's screen is a pixelated angel with a swoop of ice-cream-scoop hair. The wings only have three frames of animation, and they flap lazily. *We're full*, says the angel. *I can check your ID, but you have to wait until someone leaves*, the angel says in a pixel font that appears over its head. I look around. There is no else here except for me and the angel simulation. *I left it inside*, I say. *I left my entire wallet inside, actually. I've been in already. You checked my ID before. My credit card is at the bar. Can you let me back in? I need to get my wallet.* The angel is quiet.

I can imagine it's hard to be a bouncer for Eden, I add, trying to be empathetic. *Yeah*, the bouncer angel replies, *not really supposed to let anyone in after the last few times. People always eat the fruit, and then they dock my pay. Are you sure you've been in before?* I go to do the sign of the cross before I remember I'm not religious, so my hand just circles my chest to make an infinity sign. *Forever positive*, I say. The angel's pixels seem a little more relaxed. *Humans*, I scoff, and the angel chuckles. *Alright, get in here.* I thank the angel and say, *Selfieee*, and move my head toward the giant egg as I raise my smartphone above us to catch a good angle. The angel crosses its torch and sabre in some gladiatoresque pose.

After the angel lets me into Eden, I sit beneath a canopy of leaves, light casting through their gaps, shrubs bending around to form a bar. *Haven't seen a human in a while*, the polar bear says from behind the bar. *I'm being crucified*, I respond. *Well, you'll come down from the cross when you're good and ready*, says the bear sympathetically, and I say, *Yes, thank you.* I order one wine spritzer after another, take the fourth glass with me as I leave the bar, approaching the arboretum, where I know my tree awaits me.

The Tree of Knowledge of Good and Evil is

the most notorious. The Tree of Life has peroxide-white fruit, meaty with anemic wings. They look like terrible pigeons trying to fly away. They move, windless. Those two are the most famous of these trees. I move away from the celebrity arbors and into the lesser stock. The Tree of Honesty and the Tree of Honor. Tree of Abstention and Tree of Benevolence. Tree of Generosity and Tree of Sacrifice and Tree of Persistence and Tree of Rectitude. Tree of Sufferance and Tree of Mercy and Tree of Loyalty and Tree of Satisfaction and Tree of Compassion and Tree of Integrity. Past the Tree of Reverence there is the Tree of Happiness, which I am not permitted to eat from, yet still, it calls for me. This tree bears no fruit. It is smaller than the other trees, and glass-like, translucent. Inside, past the clear bark, there is black honey dripping and some filament buzzing like parasite.

I take out my axe from my backpack. I start to chop. A lion walks by and says, *Hey, what are you doing?* and I say, *Landscaping*, and it looks at me incredulously, but keeps walking. I wonder if someone is going to report me, if someone is going to kick me out. No one else comes, and my flawless axe swings on. It is a long time before the tree falls. The light and the Wednesday never changes. I lean against the trunk on the garden floor, sweating, taking another selfie with the fallen tree, sending a photo of it out into the digital ether.

I brush my fingers against the glossy bark. This is the thing I needed, the thing my body must be attached to. The Tree of Happiness will grow again.

I hold my faith. There are other trees, but this one is furthest away from me, and thus the one I will be crucified upon. Despite its appearance, the tree is heavier than it looks. I tie it to my back with hemp rope and walk. I bear my patibulum. *Mmmnt-mm*, a deer sasses me, shaking its head disapprovingly as I carry my burden out of the arboretum. *Sorry*, I say. *Sorry*, I say to the disappointed looking polar bear as I return my spritzer glass. *Sorry*, I say as I drag my burden past the bouncer angel as the pixels diminish. I exit Eden and the screen fades out in dejection. *Humans*, I say to the appraising air.

When I am home, it is still Wednesday. My body is ravaged, trying to recall the last time it ate. *Tell Judas I will see him in three days!* I text my cat-sitter friend. I put my phone on airplane mode. It would be rude to interrupt the process of crucifixion. Although I am back home, I do not go home. Instead, I walk atop the highest hill. With my carpenter's wisdom, I begin to hack away with my axe, making purposeful registers. The Tree of Happiness no longer looks like itself. It is amazing what you can do with a single tool. A little rustic, yes, but the parts look good. Strange angles of glass and dark goo dripping onto the grass, smothering as tar. I take out a large mallet and long spikes from my backpack. The two pieces nailed together: a cross is formed. It looks sculptural, something that could be sold in expensive art galleries. Yet, a thing with purpose.

Because I am a very do-it-yourself person, I begin to crucify myself. This ultimately doesn't matter in the end, because Roman soldiers always show up to a crucifixion to finish the job. I start like this though: the sharpest spike is pushed against the wrist. Most people never learn the proper way to crucify themselves. You don't go through the hands. You want to push the nail between your ulna and radius bones—right in the gap—so the weight of your dying body doesn't rip your hand. If you fall off the cross through torn flesh, what's the point of being crucified in the first place? A living body touching the ground during a crucifixion is worse than a flag touching the ground. Both result in flames.

No one really wants to be crucified, but it's different when you know you have to be. My incredible strength makes it easy as I suffer the nail through the left wrist with my right hand. The veins get tangled a bit, but I don't push through anything vital. It would be a shame to bleed to death when I have gotten this far. Still I bleed. The hardest part is piercing the thick skin of the other side. When the skin expands as a pyramid at the top of my left wrist, I have to move my right fingers around it. I push at the sides as hard as I can until there is a light pop and the spike has broken through completely. The thin blood goes everywhere, and I have to keep wiping to see where everything is. This is when I lie flush against the cross: the redness of me so dramatic against the clearness of the glassy wood. I take the mallet in my right hand and push the spike completely into the wood. This is the point where I am stuck, as it's very hard to nail your right wrist into a cross when your left hand is already nailed flat—but it doesn't matter—as this is always the point when the Roman soldiers show up.

After they do their job, I am high in the air, looking across the maquette-like houses on the horizon. A soldier is putting the final two nails through my feet. As I am when I am at the phlebotomist, I focus outward. The excruciating burst of the metal hitting nerves: I feel horrible electricity in me—imagine sea anemone, brutality, lightning, the shatter running through my legs and sweat upon my sweat. Something about the pain is making my brain processes go haywire. Needles. Synaptic lightning.

I can see my apartment complex from up here, I say to the only Roman soldier I know by name—Longinus. There is always a Longinus because he is the one who has to poke you at the end of the crucifixion to make sure you are dead. *Uh-huh*, he says. *I'll probably talk less from this point out*, I say. *I need to conserve my breath. It hurts to be crucified.* Longinus looks up at me. *Then shut up*, he says. He is being cold, but I know he has some affection for me; it is an important role to be able to test if someone is dead or not during a crucifixion. I have little affection for Longinus; it's his lance that matters. Gilded and sharp. *Spear, javelin, syringe, revenge*, I say in a quiet sing-song voice as the sun beats down on me. I am more delirious than I presumed I would be as I approach my death. At least I wasn't birched, although I am deserving of that too, it just wasn't in the cards. Some of the soldiers sit in the grass and play Euchre. From above, their red centurion helmets look like a drag queen's eyelashes, blinking.

The Romans perfected crucifixion, at least its capacity as a punishment that both maximizes pain and suffering. They're oh-so-particular about it too: the feet not touching holy ground, how this disgraceful death is mostly reserved for slaves and revolutionaries. I am neither. Although the Romans perfected this persecution of the body, perfection doesn't make it any less disturbing to watch. Seeing a body nailed to a cross is a horror to look upon. Because it is a horror, many spectators cry. This is the reason a weeping woman is always attracted by the act.

A weeping woman doesn't actually have to identify as a woman—"weeping woman" is certainly an antiquated and essentializing term. A lot of actors-out-of-work and drag queens take up side jobs as weeping women. My assigned weeping woman comes in a full, blue body suit. Sequined Lycra. She mirror-balls across the grass. She weeps. She resembles an old camp star with her high cyan eyeshadow. She is doing some performance art type of stretching as she cries loudly. If no one takes care of your body, it gets consumed by predatory animals. This is why weeping women are vital. They will watch you, cry for you, make sure your body is whole.

The thing is, most people assume the crucified die from starvation and dehydration, or bleeding into emptiness. This is an underestimation of the capacity for the human body to suffer. It is one's body weight that becomes totality when hung by one's own arms. Even with all my gym strength and my Pilates-earned flexibility, each breath is acute and harrowing. As I rise up to breathe, I feel the

textured walls of the spike rotating against the edges
of my bones, nerves igniting again in intensity. Me,
burning. It's the aggravation of the body's corners
that makes one want to stop, give up, prevent the self
from rising to intake one more shallow, unbearable
breath into the weakened lungs. Just when you think
you're ready to die, you rise up and open the wounds
wider.

Dried, my lips react to the abundance of light.
The sun ignites me everywhere. Longinus is moving
a sea sponge on the end of his lance. I cannot speak.
I have only three words left in me. To use that
energy.... I attempt to close my mouth, bite down
before the wet mass touches. *C'mon*, Longinus insists,
annoyed. *It's champagne. Drink it from the sponge. It will
hydrate you. You love champagne, don't you? It'll numb the
pain. It'll help.* I keep my mouth closed tight. *It's either
this or we break your legs and end this now*, Longinus
says, as if I didn't have the power to end this at
any moment. The weeping woman is bursting aural
blues—as if her teardrops were entering the air—
hitting us all. *Oh FATHER, FATHER!* she cries. *THE
FATHER! THE FATHER!* she cries again, louder. The
centurions gather beneath my feet. Longinus pushes
harder. *FATHER! FATHER! HE WHO CREATED
THE TREE OF HAPPINESS THAT YOU ARE NOT
PERMITTED TO EAT FROM!* I turn my head
slightly. Each micro-movement of the body affects it
as a whole. *Don't you like champagne*, Longinus offers
in a sweet voice. *What brand?* I gasp out in slow
hesitations. *It's André*, Longinus offers back. *Never*, I
say, and die.

When I die it goes like this for three days:

Then I return, entombed. It is no longer Wednesday. It is like waking up in a hospital, drugged through the kiss of anesthesia. There is a circular crevasse where I am, and this is the only way the light enters. I wriggle until the tight gauze wrapped around my body becomes loose. There are dried herbs between various layers of wrapping, and my body smells of thyme, garlic, rot. In the layer closest to my skin is my smartphone. I stand, and I am nude, but my muscles have returned to full form. I am hungry, but I am also full of vigor, a dizzy passion in my hands. There are holes and these holes are all over me, inside me, but I am cleansed of that life that existed before. I am famished for the unclean though, an interior space that continuously needs retribution. I crave pepperoni, mushrooms, olives, pesto, anchovy, onions. I think of Judas's soft fur between my fingers. I take a selfie with the flash. I send it to my cat-sitter friend. *Be back soon. Just was resurrected, lol.*

With all my strength I grab whatever blocks the light, some huge boulder, and I push. My feet sink into the dirt, and I push. It rolls. It is Easter. Where I am there are children with chocolate smeared across their mouths. Pastel suits in white, lavender, seafoam, pale yellow. Floral dresses. White. Plastic eggs with coins and candy hidden inside. From a distance I hear the outburst of tears again, the weeping woman has returned, coming closer in her jumpsuit, screaming, *YOU HAVE RISEN! THE FATHER! THE FATHER! THE FATHER HAS BROUGHT YOU BACK! WHAT WAS ONCE DEAD RETURNS IN FLESH ANEW!* She drops a basket of Cadbury at my bare toes. Dazed, I wish she was still—but I don't want to patronize her because, after all, we all have our roles—so instead I stand there and listen as she sings her song of the paternal, the song of the fatherly ghost.

I knew what I had to do, what the self had to do in a state of devastation, that totality, the cross through litanies, craftwork, agony. The weeping woman is here because I was crucified, and I was crucified because I had to be crucified. *It's okay*, I say. *It's okay. This was preordained.*

She replies, *NO, THE FATHER. YOUR FATHER. WE MUST GIVE PRAISE TO THE FATHER! THE ONE WHO HAS BROUGHT YOU BACK.* The sun catches the burnished plastic of a turquoise egg, a beam of light splinters, casting white beams on the grass. My stomach growls.

No, I reply, hungry and groggy. *He is not my father. I have but one father and his name is Papa John.* With this I turn, begin my walk again, move in a direction only known to me, toward that single thing I desired all along.

Moonflower, Nightshade, All the Hours of the Day

Most days I wake up at 3:00am in our shared loft. I cook myself breakfast. I bake scones. I leave snacks out for my valentine, if he is feeling well enough to eat. I bike through the city in darkness. There are party-goers with green lipstick, curled wigs, tight tube dresses; they all stumble past me as I make my way uptown toward Chelsea. I can't really consider all the drunks bumbling home, or else the ones halfway to their next party. I have to be at work by 4:30am.

The flower district is not the flower district when I store my bike in the office, but it has been working to become itself for hours. The trucks with their blinking emergency lights arrive first. Then, us with our dollies, moving orchids back and forth. The palm trees. Citrus. Bonsai, cacti, banana, fern. From light stalks to heavy ceramic pots we move in automation, turning both the inside of the store, and the storefront, and the entire edge of the sidewalk into a jungle. How strange all those soaring potted trees look under the lamp light! A single-street ecosystem with buildings and fronds scraping the underbelly of night. Then the trucks leave. Then comes dawn, and the florists, wedding specialists, and anyone else looking for an early morning deal.

I am a sales associate. I man my market. I am there to talk bloom time, haggle price, predict upcoming inventory. It all happens so quick. There is an anxiety to all the flowers being grabbed up. The customers run back and forth between all the stores that line 28th Street, trying to remember which deal is the best deal. I carry, I consult, I help them store giant bundles on our aluminum shelves. They pay in cash. The women carry stalks as tall as they are. The men in their skinny jeans and designer shoes, almost yell at me, saying these are shit prices and I know it. But we are not just American. We are Holland, we are Ecuador. We are Thailand. We are import. So they suck it up; they hand over the green for green.

Our shop usually closes by 10:30am, and I'm out an hour later. I take off my apron and fetch my bike. I always bring home flowers in its basket—sometimes stalks five yards long. There is a calculation to the balance, to keeping this all from falling apart. This time, when I bike home, the party-goers are asleep. It's the day-jobbers—those who are catching an early lunch—whom I speed past. Or else the muscle queens of Chelsea returning from the gym. Or else those who are shopping, grabbing groceries, on their way to a very important meeting. I weave through them all—past yellow medallion cabs—the tire-tread Odysseus returning to his valentine.

And there he is, in his red robe, at the metal dining table, a spoon of Greek yogurt curled beneath his bottom lip. He looks so vibrant against all the hanging plants, how our shared loft is illusioned into jungle too. Transmuted into something uncity.

"Are you feeling better, darling?" I ask, as rehearsed.

"A little bit. I think I have a sinus infection. I'm feeling dizzy and nauseous."

I kiss him on his temple.

"You're hot," I say. "I need to fill some orders, but if you get back into bed, I'll bring you an ice pack and make you some soup."

Up he rises, briefly, kissing me on the throat, on the Adam's apple, lightly biting with his canines. This is our tableau vivant, our diorama of raspberry and green. And so I laugh as actors laugh, playfully swatting him away. I unwrap the long blooming cotton stalks I brought in, lay them in bed next to him. I watch him touch the raw, unprocessed bursts as I put away the dishes.

His mother is a lighting technician who once worked on Broadway. She later moved to Chicago, where she was born, leaving the apartment to her son. It wasn't until I moved in that we decided to knock down his childhood walls, turn the space into something lush and open. Something new, defined by oxygen and green life. Something mine too. I pay the taxes, the miscellaneous fees. It works out for the both of us. He, who is always sick, cannot get a regular job. He is worried that I think he is a hypochondriac, as the tests always come out unclear. I take him to the waiting room; I sit as the blood gets sucked up, spiraling into the tube. Inconclusive. "And some days are better than others," we say as all people with an illness like this talk. Still, he is capable. He writes from his laptop. He pitches stories, think pieces; he gets paid what freelancers get paid.

I prepare myself at my perfumer's desk. It looks like a church organ, if all the vials were brass pipes lining the curved edges. My valentine got this for me on our last anniversary. Some old queen on the Upper East Side died: a local perfumer who was carried in Henri Bendel. I create blends and give them Greco-Roman names: Niobe smells briny, Persephone like daffodil and pomegranate. From the bed I hear cartoon voices, stretched flat through laptop speakers. I turn to see my valentine, his putto face laughing at some fluorescent show. Most people would use the word *cherubic*, but this is incorrect. A cherub is not baby-faced; it is a horrible winged beast with four faces: of ox and eagle and lion. My valentine is of putti, those angel children from Baroque paintings: cheeks rosy, asleep on clouds, playing tiny trumpets. I have to know my myths and my flowers because this knowledge feeds us. I wrap the ice pack in a washcloth, rest it on his forehead, above his own puffiness: those bulbous lips I love.

My fingers move as a composer's: from vetiver to leather, suede to ylang ylang, tobacco to clove to ozone. Angel's trumpet last. I am layering the notes. I fill the bottles one by one for my online shop. Most perfumers make big batches, but made-to-order is my way. It's like a shell game. Don't gamble; it's hard to follow my hands. The accords move with me back and forth to the kitchen. It's a risk, a trick, and I am exact with my fingers. I think about some future day, some big break, some A-lister buying one of my concoctions, sponsoring me, having this be my only occupation. What it would mean to work with large quantities. Celebrities. Then my mind goes back to all the things I have to do. I run to the stove, heat the water in the pot, add stock that I made from old vegetables kept in the freezer. I carry my vials and multitask. The scent of bergamot and Gaïac wood combines with chopped onions in the air—knife in my hand, it slaps against cutting board—the laughter of my valentine carries to my ears as life brings itself back into his body.

"Want to smell this one?" I say.

"You know I can't ever smell anything," he sulks in that half-congested pitch.

When I am done filling the bottles, I wash my hands over and over, carefully wrap the parfums in bubble wrap. Then, into beige boxes with my company's logo they go: the femme bloom of that vespertine flower we call datura.

"Soup's ready," I say, bringing him a bowl. He tugs at my arm.

"Get in bed," he insists.

"Did you finish writing that gossip piece you told me about?"

"Almost," he says, but there is something hungry in his voice, something wolfish. He is swaddled in the red blanket, moving his formless hands beneath to grab at me, pull me toward him.

"Well, you wrap it up and send it off. I'm going to bike down to the Post Office and get these in the mail." He leans up to bite my neck again, but I back away. "And eat your soup so you feel better."

"Okay…" he says, his firm grip not quite letting go.

When I'm back on my bike, it's 3:45pm, and I feel some wholeness to my being. If I am exact with my measurements of time it's because all obsessions should be measured exactly. I see all the people crashing from their morning coffee, rushing toward that next espresso. I see the mothers and nannies walking their children home from school. I see all the hundreds of thousands of different types of people who inhabit this city in its late afternoon.

At the USPS, I make eyes with a young man in the stamp line, or at least try to. He has thick lips like my valentine, that same pale face, rosy cheeks. Maybe this guy is just wearing blush. I make it known I am keen to the cardinal, but he won't validate me or my flirtations. It's okay. It's unusual for me to feel desirable. Spend enough time with me, though, and you'll succumb, find me infectious. Sometimes I break my stride, this bustle that keeps me efflorescent in the city. I test myself when no one I know is around. I try not to lose control, or else I fall into a hole where I think I might not know what I want. I have to stick to all these choices I have made for myself. I have to remind myself I know exactly what I want.

I was surprised, when I first met my valentine, how we ended up in the loft in the first place. We met each other around the beginning of his illness. It's a strange thing to say, a strange way to define the days, I know. I remember what his life was like before he was sick, and yes, he was always this angelic, Herculean, something. Like marrow I know he keeps me for how well I take care of him. I'm inside. Every bone needs marrow. He had self-determination before me, but now his body is one that needs me beside it to continue. The roots of banyan trees, too, grow like this.

I hate lines because my mind always returns to these places, these old anxieties. All the angelic faces of strangers. The cherubic features I hide. My valentine is leagues beyond me in terms of attractiveness. He could be in the movies, or else some prince from a picture book. A huntsman. A pirate. Something about the ratio of shoulder-to-hip, height, the size of his head in comparison. I think there is a math to beauty, and it works like this. When he is well enough to go out, when we dine at fine restaurants with red sauces, I am always jealous of the other gazes. I see them looking at him. I feel that old petty jealousy inside. It took step by step to move in with him, to bring the sledgehammer to the walls, to suspend the pothos from all those hooks, to root myself into the space where it was just much as mine as it was his. Now we are intertwined, inseparable. Like mangroves our love manacles.

The short, bespectacled postal worker takes my tiny boxes beneath the bullet-proof glass with chopsticks. He doesn't even lean forward in his ergonomic chair. I chuckle to myself as this mastery, and how well this man has figured out how to do his job with minimal effort. The peculiar things we do to make our days easier. I am the same. When I leave the Post Office, I refuse to acknowledge the faux-valentine, the rosy-cheeked incubus who I mistook for my putto. There are men like him who catch my eye, but I have one devotion, one person who I followed down city blocks for years, my kettle closing in.

The truth is: he would leave me eventually. He would find someone cuter, someone wealthier, someone younger, someone more vibrant, someone with a better job, someone with interests closer to his. This is not to say we are incompatible, only that I desired him, and I got him, and I will make sure this love maintains. When I get back on my bike and see all the life thriving in the city, I feel a sadness for my kept man. We're not stupid. I know some part of him must know, or will figure it out eventually, even as I've devised as many ways to keep this going for as long as possible. The soups. Ear drops while he sleeps. You can only be so careful, so clever. You get lazy. Small parts of you start to believe in justice, wanting him to figure out what you've been doing to him all these years. I swallow that self-destruction. I smell my fingers before I unchain my bike, lick underneath the nail with the rouge of my tongue.

"Sent!" he cheers as I unlock the door, and I cheer back, kicking off my shoes, unraveling the jeans from my legs, wrapping my cold legs around him, his feverish form heating me up inside and out. I set his laptop on the floor beside the bed and wish I could descend somewhere deeper beneath his incandescent skin. Under the duvet it's all anatomy: nipple, navel, knucklebone. I hold him in our shared bed, which sits in the middle of an open space on bleached, wooden floors. I hold him in our shared bed while all the vines and succulents surround us. And the airplants against the walls. And the peace lilies. I hold him in our shared bed while some last wisps of soup ghost through the air, while he says, "Uhh, babe, I don't feel so good." I pet his forehead and play with his hair and hold him in our shared bed while he goes to the only safe place: sleep.

I begin to descend there too, as the sun is setting, how it's after 5:00pm, and I must be in bed, as I have to rise early again. On schedule, I'll wake when the partiers are partying, scrape dry cream from bowls in the sink, finish the dishes, cook another breakfast and prepare something for my valentine too.

I hold his burning body under our red duvet in the center of the room while all the plants stare down, and my vials at the perfume desk look on as cherubs. I hold him now as I'll hold him tomorrow, and the day after that, and the day after that one. My tenderness moves like this: one hand over the mouth to feel that hotness, the heat of the body's decline. I hold him in our shared bed, my body now, too, hot, wrapped into his, and I know that he is mine, this us inside a husk, some mollusk in its bloodshell. Valentine like the white doily edge of hard paper. Valentine like my only. Like running bamboo I root myself, spread out. The saline on his skin like lachrymose. I lick, a slow peck into the warmth. The remnants of small doses—datura and DNA on my tongue. The poison this love maintains. Like this I go closer to sleep—think of a knife hitting an onion— all the volatiles gasses moving invisibly in the air.

Where Parallel Lines Come to Touch

After the funeral my brother came back. It was that same night, nearly dawn, and I was alone. I had told Mom and Dad *I'm okay* before turning in for the night, although no one had asked. It wasn't long before I left my bed to sleep in my dead brother's, which is probably not what someone does when they're *okay*. I pushed my thoughts somewhere unbrother, buried my face in my nightshirt so I'd stop smelling the grease of his hair in the pillow. I wasn't sure what I had wanted. I thought about making seagrape jelly, or else driving an hour north to the old theatre, the one where the r came before the e. They made Italian sodas there. There was a silent film they showed with a real, living organ player. It was a nostalgia, but whose?

We had to go inland to bury River, travel to drier places where the coffin wouldn't be soaked in saltmud, although most of the earth here was wet, no matter how deep you dug. The funeral home was next to an apothecary where he used to take me in his pick-up truck to buy bath bombs. The apothecary was someone else's nostalgia too, like when my mother talked about soda counters at pharmacies in the fifties. I loved soaking in baths, so River took me there at least twice a month, but I don't think I ever noticed the funeral home itself before I had to go inside it.

I thought River must have walked all the way back, that night. I was mostly asleep, but I heard him unbuckle his belt, drop his pants on the floor with a clink. I wanted to look, to see his body, make sure it was his, but the ceremony was closed-coffin for a reason. I was in the corner, facing away, almost trying to lose myself in the space between the bed and the wall because what kind of brother comes back?

We'd spent our entire lives together: sleeping, dressing, undressing, bathing. It was a two-bedroom house on stilts, an enclosed space where claustrophobia and hydrophobia came together into a marriage. People who settle on islands know they may one day be taken away by all that water, but they continue on with their hubris.

I had spent a life sharing a room with my brother—I could feel his absence. Even the floorboards creaked as he shifted his weight in the way only he could. When he slid under the comforter, he wrapped his legs around mine. They were cold and damp. I reached my hand backwards to touch the past: first the shoulder, then the tank top, which had a soft dewiness like a used washcloth.

"You came back," I said, staring straight at the wall.

"Did I go somewhere?" he said in that unchanged voice. His hand came forward, touching my stomach with a badgering prod. "Why are you in my bed? Did something happen?"

I remained quiet. There was a wistfulness in his voice—a small delight—as if maybe I had come around to something. He seemed unaware of our situation.

"Was it Dad?" He put his mouth so close to my earlobe that I could feel his lips against the little filaments that grew from my lobe.

"We fought," I said, "Something about losing...."

I couldn't. I could feel my brother pulling away, air-conditioned prickles pushing against my back in the space between our bodies.

"Losing? What does that mean?" he said in an annoyed hush, before easing back toward me. "Forget about Dad. Do you remember when you used to sneak into my bed?"

Of course I did. Our childhood was marked by the secret languages we created for one another. Our night ritual was to steal Mom's flashlight, the one in the shape of a sea turtle. We used to lie in bed creating shadow puppets, then tapping our child-fingers against the wall in our code. He reached past me, and I could see his skin in whatever light slivered its way into the night room. His flesh looked clammy as his fingers tapped into the wall, light stretching along the surface of his skin.

His fingernail dragged into an arc against the texture of the paint, then back down. He drew what looked like triangle, a lemon, an egg. He drew an invisible heart with his finger, tapping at the center three times. I repeated the gesture, tapping the center five times. River's wet hand slid over mine.

"I was just thinking: maybe I could get use my phone's flashlight against the wall, make your favorite animals."

"No," I said. "I think I'm done with those memories for tonight."

"I'm going to go sleep in your bed then," he whispered.

"No," I said again, squeezing, feeling that space between our fingers where the temperature differed.

"Moody Gourd," he said, and rested his chin on the back of my shoulder.

"*Water Otter,*" I whispered, holding his hand, afraid of what it could mean to let go.

* * *

Before the funeral, my brother had been taking what he called "a gap year," even though he was twenty and had been done with high school for two years. Isn't a gap year supposed to be singular, and then you grow up, sign up for college, go on with your life? I had, anyway, taking classes at the local community college at the south tip of the island. Mom and Dad said River was *sensitive*, which is why they never kicked him out. Or maybe that was just my projection. The truth is, you couldn't get rid of one of us without getting rid of the other. Like going to the mall on the mainland where the dressing rooms have a mirror on each side—projecting yourself forever—River and I were like this.

I was just weeks from being done with my associate's, and River had his job as this inventory-auditor person. Combined, we were enough of an adult, a person made whole, although the truth was we'd always both been seen as immature. Even in our somewhat continued adolescence, we tried to become complete. River held his job, going out at dawn to the three grocery stores on the island, and then he continued outward: driving his pick-up truck along the bridge toward all the other stores on the mainland. He had this barcode scanner that he'd bring with him to the water aisle. His job was exclusively to audit the water. *Wa-ter Au-di-ter*. The syllables were liquid too; how clumsy they fell from my mouth.

* * *

When I woke up alone, the sky filtering grey early-morning light through the curtains, I knew there was only one place he could be.

I put on my black-and-white striped leggings, my Mary Janes with a cute cat face on the tip of each shoe. I slid a black velour dress over my body: the one with long, flowy sleeves. It was almost December, and the gulf breeze held a slight bite to it. Now that the tourists were gone, there was a coldness that would sink into anything. It was red tide season too, that mysterious time when the water turns to blood and all the dead fish spill out on the shore. Combined with the unseasonable early winter winds, the only people left here would be locals—and maybe a few tourists who were really, really bad at planning vacations.

In our kitchen, Mom was shoveling some sad eggs on a piece of toast. Dad was a few feet behind her, scrubbing the frying pan.

"Does River work at Paul's Grocery first on Saturdays?"

They shot each other a look.

"Sorry—*didn't* River work Saturdays? At Paul's Grocery?"

"I don't understand the tenor of this conversation," my father said, sharply.

"Riley," my mom said, trying to conceal entire sentences in the five letters of my name.

My father shook the steel wool in his hand at me. "It's been one day since we said goodbye, Riley. We just had a nice breakfast too." I stared at the bits of yellow caught in the silver. He looked up and down my outfit. "Can't you at least act normal?"

"What are you talking about?" I said, indignant.

"She's mocking us," he said to my mother. "Look at you. What are you wearing? Maybe you could cut the death cult get-up given our family's situation."

"I'm *mourning*," I said. "It's what people do when their loved ones die. They wear black." I went over and kissed my mom on the cheek. "*Sorry*," I whispered to her. "I'll be home for dinner."

"You've been in mourning long before—long before—your *mourning* clothes are just going to keep upsetting your mother," my dad said, turning to face the sink again, to put extra elbow grease into the sud-soaked pot he had moved onto. My mother was already cooing to diminish his anger. I wonder if there was a part of me she hated as much as I hated the part of her that continued to stay with him?

The fight from the previous night had been awful. All three of us screamed after everyone had left. It started with Dad though. When he spoke of *loss*, as if it was his alone, I felt so small, parts of me disappearing into cellophane. It had almost come to blows, but my father had never hit my mother, and I seemed to exist, at least tenuously, in the same world she did. I knew the morning would bring a familial reset button of last-night-never-happened, although now I wanted to run away more than ever. Or was I too old to *run away?* As a twenty-year-old wouldn't it, instead, simply be *leaving* or *living?* With my forthcoming degree, there were four-year universities, possibilities. I could move away from my father, into a future where I was always this Riley.

I waved my middle fingers at Dad's back. Whatever wonder had been inside me upon awakening had swirled down into a hot cat piss mood. I stomped back to the bedroom, shoving my daily talismans into my PVC bat-shaped backpack: a half-smoked pack of Parliaments, my lucky lighter with a pin-up model down the side, dark maroon lipstick, orange Tic-Tacs, unruly wads of petty cash, my metal water bottle covered in band stickers. When I passed our mantle next to the stairs, I saw the framed photo I had turned down last night after the fight—pointed up-right again. It's a photo of two children in matching blue overalls, matching faces. Their bowl-cuts are twinned too. *River*. I slid open the zipper of the bat bag and threw the gilded frame in, although it was an outsider amongst all my favorite possessions.

"At least my grieving process doesn't involve making everyone else around me feel like shit," I said to Dad, passing the kitchen table again, firing back my delayed comeback, making sure I was close enough to the kitchen-side door, close enough to the mathematics of escape before I popped my white-hot mouth off.

Dad was already abandoning his station at the sink, beginning to wave his finger and shout, but I was already two steps ahead, out the kitchen-side door, onto wooden staircase, trotting down as he screamed for me to *come back right this instant*.

"RIVER IS DEAD," I screamed back at the house. "FUCK YOU." I alternated these phrases as if I were leading a dark cheer, running toward my bike—"RIVER IS DEAD"—hopping onto the seat—"FUCK YOU." I pedaled fast onto the coquina-lined alley, toward the main avenue painted in tropical pastels, feeling the chubby plastic wings of my backpack bounce as I accelerated away.

I wasn't about to go around asking people if they'd seen my dead brother, although that's the type of thing that everyone would think I would do. I'm not even *that* weird. I had a job this past summer. I was a lifeguard on the beach: wore that alarm-red one-piece, traded in my black-and-white-polka-dot monokini for nine dollars an hour. I took one class in the evenings where most of my classmates ignored me. When you look like Halloween in a beach town, it stands out against everything that is day: the perpetual Fourth of July that haunts everyone.

Even if I may still act like a brat sometimes, might get mistaken for teen more than most, I didn't start dressing this way until I got to community college. Before, when I was in high school, there was one girl in my grade who wore black fishnet, plaid skirts, pierced her ears with safety pins. I wanted to be her for so long. Back then I was all baggy shirts, unmemorable jeans. My parents controlled every aspect of my life up until then, down to what I was allowed to eat, read, wear. They managed the where and whens of my schedule immaculately. It was easy to behave, to go along with my curated life, when it was so small, surrounded by all this water.

River used to play the role of the punk, before he became obsessed with adulthood. Though, had he fully changed? Even as an adult he'd wear black polo shirts to his water auditor job, a contrast against all the peaches-and-cream motels, neon palm trees— the soundtrack of steel drums that follows you everywhere. River was the bad twin, the one who went through his angst phase unquestioned. Back then, he had liberty spikes—dyed blue—and none of his clothes fit just right. He wore dog collars until twelfth grade—like an actual dog collar he got at PetSmart with a custom tag that said *Fuck the Police*. He used to sneak out, ride to the mainland to see punk shows. He never got in trouble either. He could be as bad as he wanted; I had to be responsible, the senior who skipped senior skip day. Then, as soon as we graduated, River changed his shtick, dressed like he was selling door-to-door life insurance. Maybe when he stopped being that River, it gave me permission to start being my Riley.

Now Mom and Dad treat me like I'm some new, peculiar thorn that's grown on a flower they used to know. But the flower was always a rose, always had thorns. They don't realize the voice they slip into: the one that tells their idealized version of me what I do or do not know about the world. I'll refuse them. I'll continue to be my Riley, continue to be how I always wanted to be. Even in the cheesy black garb, I know I'm reclaiming some part of my past, trying to know myself fully. It's not like I'm unaware how ridiculous I look, clad in dark velour, peddling on a child's bike across the width of a tropical island. Perhaps if I had learned to drive properly when I turned sixteen, I could have gone to the mainland more often, exposed myself to something bigger, changed faster, become this Riley sooner. Maybe I secretly liked the constraint, back then, because it meant I didn't have to change. I could go as far as my bicycle took me, and that was enough.

* * *

I checked the small parking lot for River's truck, but it wasn't there. Of course it wasn't. Still, I wanted to go inside the store, walk to that aisle, to check for him. As I passed the bike rack in front of Paul's, I noticed a dead grouper leaned over the metal. How had it gotten there? Had it died in the red tide? Who had abandoned it on the rack? Its eyeball had fallen out, and I stared at the hole in its head while fidgeting with my bag—before realizing I forgot my U-Lock.

I walked my bike inside the grocery with me. I had to navigate a carton of broken eggs while I looked for him, narrowly missing the yolk with my tires. I was both surprised and unsurprised there was a mess, uncleaned. Although island towns are small towns, they're unpredictable with the way people come and go. People were mostly gone: on the beach, in the grocery. So, it's not like I thought anyone would steal my bike, but it was also all I had left, so there was no other option but to keep it by my side. The few employees I passed—most of them who went to my high school—looked at me like they wanted to say something, but most just looked away.

I heard that noise first: the familiar beeps. That sound of a red crosshair of light sliding down the jail cell of the barcode. When I turned the corner, there he was: black hair parted to the right, face completely intact. It was like God hit a reset button too. That face pained me beyond anything. River worked the angles so he could scan the cylindrical VOSS bottles without even turning them to get the labels.

"Water Otter," I said. River looked over at me, doing his trademark casual half-wave.

"Life Gourd," he smirked, pausing to finish the row. "You picking something up for Dad?" he asked.

"Are you kidding me? Dad is being a raging ass again. I'm not doing shit for him."

"What happened this time?" he said, eyeing the bike by my side, crouching, moving toward the Fiji. River was always focused when he did his job, but there was a confusion on his face then too.

"Nothing! I think he's just taking his anger out on me—taking it hard that—it's just that—I—"

I moved my hand, pressed my fingers into his clavicle—it felt like the toughest part of his body—calcium and diamonds, a hardness. How could I tell him our fight was about him? I never thought I'd be in the position to tell the dead they were dead, but River was here, and all I could do was stutter and prod. Even in his wholeness, his aliveness, something about him felt dreamed, as if I had just woken him up from a deep sleep. Something was wrong about his return, though, and it was hidden in the body of my twin.

"Don't you remember last night?" I asked him, slightly pleading.

"You slept in my bed last night, Gourdy Gourd," he said, remembering, now putting his hand against my collarbone. We were reflections operating on a lag. One of the fluorescent overhead lights caught his eye, and he looked dizzied. He looked back at me, smiling, as if trying to recall what we were talking about.

"You'll have your associate degree in a few weeks. Don't worry. You'll get a job, I'll still have a job, then we can move away together, pay for a nice apartment. No more fights with Dad. You don't have to talk to me about yesterday's fight—or today's—if you don't want to. Just focus on the future. We'll leave together." He smiled that River smile again. My smile.

Yes, leaving together had been our plan, before I was thrust into a reality where I'd have to do it without him. Or was there no thrusting? Hadn't I always secretly imagined leaving them all, going off alone? I swallowed a lump in me, trying to displace all my feelings about River's revival. I hated the thought of leaving Mom alone with Dad, but I needed to get away, and the fantasy of doing it with River had made everything feel possible. Possibly possible. At least part of the time. The truth is, perhaps, that River would never understand why the plan was imperfect, what it would mean to continue living *with* him. This was the fracture in our minds, where River thought everything was simple, attainable. He made moving through the world sound so easy. He believed you could just become the *you* that you always wanted to. Just like that. Unlike him, fantasies of change bogged me down, swallowed me whole.

"I saw a job out West, another beach town. A fancy restaurant. They needed a water sommelier," he said. "You could get a life-*gourding* job again."

"When did you see that job listing?" I asked, slightly annoyed. His mouth opened to speak, but then dropped again, his bottom lip curled inside, teeth biting down onto flesh. His face was alarming to watch. It wouldn't be the first time I opened my mouth and immediately regretted what I had said.

"Uhh, when are you off for lunch?" I blurted, grabbing his shoulder, trying to change the subject. "We could get Skinnie's? It'll be my treat!"

River shook his head. "We had a burger yesterday," he said matter-of-factly, distracted from the previous job inquiry.

"Yesterday...?" I had asked about the job listing to test his memory, his sense of time. We had eaten a burger together, that much was true, but that was already eight days ago. It took a week to recover the body, to prepare it, to bury it. Contents of the gut: cheeseburger with a fried egg on top, ibuprofen, salt water, rum. The funeral was yesterday.

Since he crawled into his bed with me the previous night, I became dazed under the spell of my brother's mere presence, in the belief that he had returned. I came to his work because I needed to know his body was bound by gravity like mine. Bound by water. Blood. Land. He was beneath the land, leaving my body on top, leaving my body up here on the island, alone. What would the world think of me now that I was untwinned? Growing into being the bad twin was easy, but the bad only child? But I wasn't alone, was I? He was still here. Existing. Reminding.

"Did you drive here?" I asked, anxious.

"Of course, I..." but he trailed. There was something childlike to his face, as if I had asked him a riddle. Why did I ask him that? What did I truly want?

"Never mind. Do you need a ride?" I asked.

"Did you borrow Mom's car?" he replied, still

mulling over something that only he was unsure of.

"I biked," I said, making an obvious motion toward the bike I held with a hand.

"Right," he said, mind half-elsewhere.

"You can ride on the pegs," I said. "It will be like those times."

"Those times," he said back, returning to his work, scanning the final Fiji barcode. "Okay. We can do Skinnie's. I'll finish my inland work later."

He slid the barcode scanner back in his holster, like he was from another time, another region where cowboys rode seahorses, patrolled lands that were underwater, forever wet.

Outside, I took off my bat bag, put it over his shoulders. If it stayed on my back, the hard wings might prod him in the chest as we rode. When he put his hands on my shoulder, I got us off to a good start, pedaling hard. The breeze hit softer with the weight of an extra body, but I imagined him back there, balancing on the pegs, some type of bat angel sent from Bat Heaven. He was sent to Human Earth as a tourist, and I was showing him around for the first time. Only then did it seem like everything started to move faster.

* * *

I always suspected Dad loved River more. Mom, me. At least before I became brattier, more indignant. These things are hard to prove, but you can see it in the little moments—the way Dad would pat River's back as we got ready for school on those mornings, or the way Mom would tenderly clean out my ears with a Q-Tip after some of my baths. The four of us became more distant after high school ended. I try not to think of catalysts. People drift. Can't time be enough of a thing to blame, or is that too abstract? It was like we lived in this tiny world on four different clocks.

The night River disappeared, the police said it was *an accident*—but an accident implies something light, something impermanent. I thought about the three of us: Mom, Dad, me. How hard it would be. How fucked a trinity could be. I only prayed during really bad stomach aches, or that exam when I stayed up watching *Law & Order* instead of studying. When I approached God, I approached him like I do the librarian. This is just a lending, a book I know I will have to give back. I know I don't own this.

Still, I was incomplete without my twin brother. That night, I stayed up all night in a fever, praying. I asked God to pull him out of the gulf. I asked God to give him back to me.

It was an activist from a sea turtle non-profit who found his body. She said it was a rare sight: baby turtles had hatched near the dunes, and they followed the light of the moon down to the shore. That's where she saw him, lying in the sand, as the babies moved around the obstacle of his body into their new, aquatic world. Was it wrong, when she came to our front door with the police, that I only asked her about the turtles, why didn't she stop them from going into the harmful waters?

It was red tide, yes, but what could the activist do? The babies would live, or they would die.

The night of the burial, before the fight, but after the funeral, after the wake, after everyone had left our house, after I got out of the bath with my skin smelling of coconut and pine, I had wrapped the white towel in that perfect position—where the cotton bottom ended at the top of my thighs, leaving my legs fully exposed to the cold, air-conditioned house. Mom was in the living room, gazing out toward the dark street, toward the sound of the water, although there was no water in sight. I asked Mom if she could clean out my ears, although I hadn't made a similar request since I was fifteen or sixteen years old. She turned, looked at me like I was a stranger, and returned quietly to whatever lie beyond that glass.

* * *

It wasn't really morning any longer, but neither was it noon. I took the bat bag back from River to get my wallet out, sliding the straps so they hung off my arm at the elbow. There was only one man, named Carlos, seated at a table by himself, sipping a Corona beside some fries he wasn't eating. The screen door of the burger shack was propped open, something freshly dead coming in through the breeze.

"Hey Carlos," my brother said, nodding. Carlos did not acknowledge, did not nod back. Carlos was fond of my brother, I knew this. I also knew something else then, the way my brother moved through the restaurant, unseen.

When I pushed in front of River to the counter, reminding my brother that it's on me. Skinnie— overhearing this at the cash register—said, "Who else would it be on?"

"You think she still has a job? She's the only twenty-year-old I know with allowance money," River *tsked*, swatting my hair, the bun bobbing and the stray strands flying up.

I got it. River, of course, didn't. Skinnie knew something inside himself that he didn't quite have words for. The air was different. I could tell he sensed it, but couldn't sense *what*, but he kept staring at me, trying to pin-point my face. He looked me over again, and said, "Oh—OH."

I didn't come in Skinnie's often. I usually waited outside with my bike while River ordered. I don't think Skinnie realized who I was right away, what I was connected to.

"*It's on me,*" Skinnie whispered, tobacco and orange juice on his breath. "*Tell your folks I'm sorry. You all come back in here soon, entire family meal on me,*" he smiled through crooked teeth. It's that momentary kindness that happens at times like this, some good will that comes from a place of pity. I tried to smile back, but I wonder how awkward and monstrous my face looked to him.

When we were walking out, Skinnie shouted at Carlos to close the front door he had left open. "I hate red tide," he said. "Hate the air it brings in."

There was this private resort with its little

manmade alcove not too far from the jetty. I had forced River to wear the bag again as we got back on the bike. Maybe I liked the way it grounded him, made him cuter and bound him to this earth. My twin brother, my bat angel. I wondered if the few people who saw us only saw the dark bag hovering miraculously in the air a foot behind me as I biked. It certainly felt like I was the only person in the world who could see him. When we got close to the beach again, we walked past the manicured sea oats, the sand so white it was blinding. Condos and margaritas, dancing and bleached towels: that kind of place. They would chase us away when it was tourist season. It was down to the sixties now though, and the resort was mostly closed. The two of us had dragged white beach chairs away from luxury properties, took them to our hiding spot out by the water.

We quietly sat with our burgers, watching dead fish float onto the edge of the rocks, or else the shore. I sat in amazement watching him take a bite, watching food enter his mouth, his body.

"Did I do something wrong?" River asked loudly. "I feel like something fucked up happened, and I can't remember what. Did something happen?"

"No."

"I felt like Skinnie and Carlos were mad at me. They wouldn't even acknowledge me, man. It was rude."

"You didn't do anything," I said. "It's red tide, you know? It's like the full moon. It messes everything and everyone up."

Island people are superstitious: the full moon, gravity, what it does to the water, the tides, and yes, red tide, what it does to the fish. What the fish do to humans. A cycle, all of it. Water and waves.

River nodded, and then at least pretended not to be bothered by going unacknowledged by the gruff townies who adored him more than anyone.

We finished our burgers, fiddled with our fries, watched a half-dead pufferfish float up into the cracks of a jetty that lined the nearby shore with rocks. It spikes expanded, compressed.

"Dad used to give me shit too," River said, "I know you didn't think he did, but he did. Still does. Yeah, I know he does it to you too. The black clothes. Your eyeliner. Don't worry about it too much. You'll grow out of it, but you don't have to change. Even though you get the brunt, I haven't changed that much. I only started wearing shit like this for the job. I get it, you think I sold out, but I'm still like you on the inside. You think we're different now, that you're always in the hot seat, but it's not like that."

"Right," I said, somewhat coldly. River was the older twin by only a minute, but the way he talked you'd think he had two, three years on me. "It's always about the clothes and only the clothes."

"It's not about the clothes—but," he said, tugging at his polo, "I'm just saying this isn't me. This is for work. I'll get a better job someday, be able to wear whatever I want. Unless I sell out, of course. What do you think a water sommelier wears? A vest? A bowtie? Do you think I'll be wearing suits ten years from now?" he chuckled to himself.

Bah was the sound I made, some involuntary gasp. I couldn't stop myself. It was like my cheeks filled with air, launching an invisible jawbreaker out of my mouth. I bawled. I cried down my velour, into my basket of French fries.

River is dead. Fuck you.

His arms were coming over, scooping me up by the waist. No, I thought, trying to focus on the water, focus outside of my body, which was giving everything away.

"You're real," I said, squeezing him all over. "I hate it."

"What?"

"I was selfish," I said, crying harder. I was unruly—I had to tell him. "I asked God to take you away. OK? I'm tired of lying to myself. I did it. I said a prayer. I hated looking at your face." I struggled to get away from him. "I meant it for one microsecond, but then I didn't. I tried to take it back, but the prayer was already gone."

My brother hushed me, holding me tighter.

"You're allowed to hate me. I know I don't stick up for you as much as I should."

I tried to push him back, some inhuman screech exiting my body, as if a ghost had lived in me for years, finally free.

"No! No! No!" I screamed, petulant. "Don't you get it? I don't hate you! I've never hated you!"

Whatever I hated was just coincidence, just an accident. I just wanted to be untethered by twindom, to get on with my life alone. It felt like, back then, if he could just painlessly evaporate, even for a little bit, it would be enough that I could surpass this world without him.

"And we didn't eat burgers yesterday," I burst out, crying into his shoulder, harder, as his sturdy hands prevented me from moving away.

"I'm...confused," he said, unsure of what me wishing him dead-ish had to do with week-old burgers or him standing here now. I wrapped my hands around his ribcage, held him tighter, until I could feel the texture of his thin bones pressing into mine. Hardness. Calcium. Diamonds. My identical. My only. I moved one hand to his wrist, the other to the pulse of his neck. I felt and felt and felt, and still, there was nothing. I returned my arms around his neck as his grip on my waist refused to soften.

"Why didn't you drive to work, River?" I said, exhausted and sad and angry. "Where did you come from when you found me in your bed last night? What is your last memory? Where is your phone? Why don't you have your phone?" I was mumbling into his polo collar, but I knew he could hear me, could understand what all this meant. I tried to stifle my tears. "Don't you remember what happened to your truck? Don't you remember the bridge?"

We stood in the alcove, listening to the tired waves bring their dead to the earth. It was wrong. The fish had no place on the sand. "Oh," he said. "Oh," he said again, his breath pressed into my neck.

"I begged for you," I said, the two of us seated again, holding hands. "I asked God to give you back. I asked God to take me instead. I asked God to take

Dad. I asked God for one week. I asked God for the rest of your life. I even told God to rewind time before any of this. It wasn't a request. I demanded it. Then I asked God for the future. I would give back my body for you, River. I thought of everything we could still do, and it worked, you came back. It was so much bigger in my head. You would come back, and it would all be different, but I'm still here, and you *did* come back, and we're doing the same stupid shit that we always do." I felt dizzied by the inscrutable logic of the dead.

"It's not stupid," he said, trying to make sense of everything. "I love you. You're my twin," he said. "I am incomplete without you." It sounded so flat, so trite, but the hardest part for me was that I knew he meant it. He was sincerer than I could ever be, even in his platitudes.

"Sometimes I feel like I'm incomplete *with* you," I said in a hoarse whisper. "I don't know. I don't fully understand my feelings." There was a pause between the two of us. The pufferfish on the edge of the rocks deflated and stayed that way.

"Do you think I should come home," he said. "Should I go see Mom and Dad? Do you think they'll be able to see me? Do you think only you can see me?"

"I don't know," I said. "I don't know the rules—didn't make them—couldn't tell you. I was afraid once you found out you came back, that you would go again. I don't understand how this works. You look exactly like you did before.... Do you even want to see Mom and Dad?" My eyes were already welling up again.

"No," he said. "If I came back, I came back for you." River stood up, stretched, walked over to the water, stuck his hand in. "I guess I just forgot my purpose." The plastic wings bobbed behind him.

"Don't do that!" I said, wiping my tears. "Red tide is gross. Bacteria. Virus, something."

"Something," he echoed, but then looked down at the pufferfish. "Why do I feel so drawn to the water?"

"You know why," I said, stiffly, using my own hands to hold my ribcage this time.

"I feel like I need to return to it, to go under it. It's like there's this little insect in my head flying around, buzzing in a tiny voice, telling me to go back."

"Shouldn't you go back to your coffin then?" I said, not really wanting to negotiate any of this.

"I don't know where that is," he said. There was a pained expression on his face, like he remembered something. It hurt to see that face. I made prayers and wishes without comprehending how little I knew about what it meant to ask God for a favor. "I think I'm supposed to go back to the water."

"When?" I said, getting up, moving closer to him. "I want you to stay."

"Is that true?" he asked, turning around to face me. His face would always be this age, this youthful, this boyish. He would be *this* forever, and I would become an old woman, haunted by him, having to look into this young face for the rest of my life, knowing I had made an evil prayer and had it answered. Didn't the annulment go through, at least partially? Didn't I get him back? Is it true, me wanting him back, wanting him to stay?

"No," I said, "It's not true," moving my lips in to kiss him at the corner of the mouth, giving him back to God.

River took my hand, pulled me along all of a sudden, away from the alcove, toward the wet sand where the bodies of dead fish formed shapes, designs, unknown satellites of the gulf. We walked as far as the beach would go, to an unpassable jetty. The winter winds picked up. The rocks were slippery and high and the waves slapped on with such violence. Many people had drowned here; it was the truth of the island. All islands. Many people died other ways, but most fell into the water; it took them in, held them.

In front of us, the red waves smacked louder. There were already rows of kelp moving forward, toward us in the foam. When the water pulled back, the long algae moved into their verticals, the black lines of seaweed forming a grid on the surface of the gulf.

"This is the spot," he said. He slid his shoulders back, handing my bat bag back to me.

"Wait!" I shouted, unzipping, rummaging through it. I handed him the gilded picture frame.

He smiled a sad smile, moving his finger along the bevel of the gold-leafing. "Why was this in your bag?" he asked.

"Impulse."

"Little voice?" River said. "Glad you're

listening to it. You know my dresser?"

"In our bedroom?"

"Your bedroom," he said. "If you take the bottom drawer out there's a gap. I was hiding cash there. I thought you would have figured it out. I even hid it in front of you."

I hadn't noticed. How many days had I refused to see that face?

"It should be enough."

"Enough?" I said. Could I go away? Could I be all of myself? I looked down at the frame in his fingers.

"I'll take them with me," he said, tapping his nails against our baby faces, those children trapped behind glass. He moved in, to hold me. "Sister," he said, kissing me in that spot, giving me back to the earth. I felt the echo of our bodies again, moving through a strange mixture of duration, endurance.

When we were done, when our bodies were untouching, he removed his scanner from his cowboy holster beside him, moved his red crosshairs a final time, hovering the uneven light. Its redness disappeared in the sibling color of the waters. The kelp was still on the salt and blood of the gulf, resembling a barcode with its parallel lines. *Beep*.

Seaweed stood in its proportional bobs before coming alive, starting to slither beneath the cold, sick water as serpents do. As the greenness moved aside, bubbles rose from the water. For a moment, I thought I saw something dark and round moving beneath the seaweed. A sea turtle? Or? Whatever it was, it was gone beneath bubbles, parting waves.

Someone else was auditing, counting the dead, bringing back the one who got away for an ebb. Perhaps there are none who sneak away—only ones who are lent. I looked at my brother's face again, just once, so I could hold him in me. A flow. Then, I let go. I was whole. The gulf opened, this time, in an embrace, and my brother moved toward it, to feel it, so he, too, could be whole again.

* * *

At home, it was the evening of kept promises. I was in time for dinner: something citrus was electrifying the air inside the kitchen. Mom was at the counter, removing a pit from an avocado with a large knife. I sidled up beside her.

"Are we having ceviche?" I asked. My mother smiled at me. Ceviche was one of my favorite foods. The rest of my family had a distaste for it, for the rawness of the fish. It always felt funny, to grow up in a place like this, and be part of a family who hated eating fish. Why now? It seemed especially awful to consider flesh, but here she was, smoothly cutting the slices out of the avocado, setting them delicately on the dish. I just stood there quietly, standing next to her as she prepared three plates.

She opened one more avocado, took a half, poured ikura from a bowl into the gap the removed pit left behind. The salmon roe glistened, the orangeness of each egg catching sunset light from beyond the kitchen window.

"Eat," she said, pushing the avocado half

toward me. As I munched away at the umami bursts of the eggs against my tongue, she started up, as if delivering a small speech that I suspected she had been practicing all day. "Grief is complicated. I want you to remember we love every part of you, and that we're proud of your smarts, your degree."

"I haven't gotten it yet, Mom. And I still have two more years of college to do."

"Riley, you need to make space for the little victories. Even if I feel heavy—heavier today than yesterday—I want you to know that I'm here for you. I can still feel pulled down by grief and lifted by my love for my daughter."

I nodded, not knowing what to say.

"It's going to be hard, just your father and I, but we want you to be happy."

I nodded. She nodded, her knife hand moving on to cut a new lime.

"Forgive your father, and forgive me, if we act a certain way. This is going to take a long time before it gets easier. No one is prepared to lose one of their children. And I know," she said, moving in to caress my chin, "that no one is prepared to lose their twin." She still had the knife in her hand when she touched my face, and a small part of the cold metal touched me too.

During dinner, no one fought. No one protested the raw fish. No one brought up my obscene temper tantrum from the morning. I understood what this gesture meant, what my mother was trying to say. Dad barely made eye contact, but he didn't make any disparaging remarks either. No one mentioned River. He wasn't gone from them, but they were displacing him, if only for the night. I had heard this thing, that sometimes grieving families will continue to set a place for the dead at meals, but I was glad when we only had the trinity of plates between us.

There are nights when it's so quiet, you can hear the sound of the gulf rustling, even from the center of the island. It was one of those nights when the waves came with their soft crashes, came with whatever things still lived and hid beneath their surface. I thought of those baby turtles, then. If this was our moment of silence, so be it.

The money was exactly where River said it was. I slid the drawer out and found his hidden space. With the money removed, I decided to replace it with an offering. I took off my black velour dress, folded it into a tight square, before restoring the drawer over that dark place where I gave my alms.

I sat on my computer for hours, with the lump of saved cash in my naked lap, making plans, looking at apartments, at colleges, preparing futures where I would go off to places that didn't touch water. Although, didn't everywhere touch water?

It was long after everyone went to bed— or I thought they did—that I walked through the house nude, drawing my nightly bath. I tried to be economical with my decadence, but I felt guttered, so I used a bath bomb that River had bought me.

We had gone to that apothecary the day before he died. He had called in sick to work so we could see a black-and-white film where a hypnotist used people to commit murder. We passed the store on the drive home; I begged him to go inside. I was so sugar-high from an Italian soda, which I'm pretty sure was just seltzer and grenadine. River asked me twice if I was wearing lipstick, but I didn't know what he was talking about, because I wasn't, so I didn't answer. While I browsed, he watched himself in an ornate mirror, juggling three bath bombs, much to the annoyance of the shopkeeper. When I came up behind him, I saw the drink's red dye on my lips. The two of us in the reflection: we could have been strangers. It was later, in the car, when he handed me the tiny bag, the round, hard surface inside. I hadn't even seen him purchase it.

Lost, again, in myself, I unwrapped the chalky orb in the tub. Its surface was Christmas green, but as it dissolved into the water, it turned the tub into a burgundy, resembling wine. Of all the miracles of the world, this one was minor.

After I put on my lotion, applied a menthol eye cream that soothed the gloom beneath my eyes, slipped back in my white towel—wearing it the way I liked to wear it—I walked into the living room, seeing the back of my mother's head. She was looking down from our house that sat high on its stilts, looking through the glass, down at the street. It was too dark to see all the pastels, all the coquina, all the other houses, or the night sky, or the water. I tried to sneak past, but she must have seen me in the reflection.

"Riley," she said, "Do you need me to clean out your ears?"

"No," I replied, but I stalled, eventually moving forward, dragging a chair over to sit beside her. It was there I leaned my head on her shoulder, looked out the window to see what she had seen.

Night Things

He dreamed of water in all scales. Unlucid, he moved where sleep took him, between wetlands and underwater caverns, beach dunes and rivers. In creeks, gators floated low in mastered stillness, incised eyes reflected by boat lights. Down by the gulf, casinos of mangroves gripped mud-deep with their roots. In swamps, will-o-the-wisps buzzed as filament in cracked lightbulbs, ghost orbs pulling him down to wet murk. Salt, blue, blur, phantasmagoria advancing him from aquascape to aquascape. The seas changed again, but still he stood at the edge of the water, this one pitch-dark, sunless. He feared the black water, and then he was in it, the nightmare teleporting him, nameless things now swimming beneath him. He could not see them, but his dream-brain knew they were there, lurking in that lack of light, in the unknowable depths, their invisible mandibles reaching up toward his legs. Then, a cry, circular in its *ahh, ahh, ahhs*, penetrated his sleep until he found himself awake, vertical, frantic, looking out his bedroom window at the new moon.

It barely popped from the sky, stranger than the moons seen from his condo back in the city. He was inside some hyperreality sold as *being closer to nature*. Didn't the fact that the government owned this land mean it was no different than metropolis?

Was this acreage really other, removed from empire? Did nature even exist anymore—if it ever did? The Everglades seemed wild enough, especially when held up against Miami. Out here, the stars were now known, named.

He had been awarded a writing residency at the water's edge. He thought he could indulge in the fantasy of being away from noise and lights before he arrived—before the land swallowed. He was crafting a thriller about a pet snake, abandoned in a bog, grown too long, its open mouth as large as a dinner plate. It was eating children. The people of the town were looking for a serial killer, a man. They never expected a snake! His agent loved it. This locale was research. The sparse row of bungalows surrounded by swamp created an unkind tableau. Although owned by the National Park Service, the buildings seemed powerless against the wilderness. Human habitation was nothing, just a blip in the wetland. It felt like the swamp grass might overtake him if he turned his back to it long enough, that he might wake up with dank things slithering against his leg beneath the covers. Fangs devouring him whole. Each night, he wound down toward sleep in this state of terror. What better way to create a murder mystery than by telling yourself it would happen to you?

And now, awake again, the clean chalkboard of night alarmed him; the same darkness, lightless as the oceans of his sleep, appeared before him. There was a cloud of crickets somewhere in the grass below and behind him the heavy clicking of a fan. He had to get untangled from these sheets. He fumbled his feet and fingers, flicked the light switch on. It was four in the morning somewhere between summer and fall. The cry from before occurred again. The strange caws that awoke him were not part of the dream where danger was negligible. He focused on the cry, how it existed outside unconsciousness. The man felt calmer to be away from the bed, but bothered by this phantom bird: fleshed and feathered and somewhere in the Everglades, as far from sleep as he was.

In the kitchenette, he listened to the spoon strike clean against the ceramic cereal bowl. There was a small pleasure in all the noise he created in the quiet of each tiny room. Noise he could control. Usually, at this hour, back in Miami, he heard the wails of all the drunks being exorcised from bars. Knocking over trashcans, shouting in vodka glossolalia. But here, he only had himself, his quietude. The ears were primordial though, always listening for predators in darkness. The presence of his laptop warded the threat of being so far from others. Electricity pushed back against all that was primeval. His loud fingers clacked against the keys, as if technology only made the magic shield stronger. Why did he need a magic shield though? Weren't there only a few other occupied buildings near his bungalow? Weren't there other people, proving he was not alone in these subtropics? And, anyway, what could actually harm him? The walls were caulked, he made sure. The door was locked and locked again. Nothing could get in that he did not invite in. The man's thoughts turned to dark water, then to the swamp outside, then to his neighbors, then to The Witch—who he was trying not to think of—then to his snake pushing through a window screen and approaching a crib. A crib? What did the crib look like? What material was it made out of?

With a spoon in one hand and his other fingers tracing the keyboard, he went to work. The glowing white page of the document reminded him more of the moons he knew: full, aglow. His thoughts went from moons to snakes then birds. The bird! Every few words the bird would alert him of its presence again. He tried to ignore the whoops and whistles, the occasional arpeggios of the avian mystery. The man was struggling to solely be aware of the page before him. He moved through the same words over and over again in a circle, like the Ouroboros that eats itself forever. He focused on the act of focusing. Is this what it meant to meditate? The snake was mythological, prehistoric, growing wings, sinking teeth into its own tail. He minimized the writing before him, pulled up a search engine, entered *night birds* into the computer. The screen returned to him answerless.

The noises were more frequent, an entire score composed for him. The high notes as he spritzed bug spray along the length of his arm, the lows as he refilled batteries in the tube of the flashlight. He knew the squawks of frogs and the child-like cries of peacocks. He knew the banshee barks of red foxes. He did not know this. Was it injury or ecstasy? He had read about a mockingbird's nocturne, a song seldom heard, and only when one bird had lost its mate. It could have been a whippoorwill, but those were known for saying their own names over and over. This was not them. He rattled the flashlight against his thigh until the beam blinked on. He tugged at the invisible string on his finger, attaching him to whatever bird talked through the distance of night.

The driveway was a long gradient of gravel to dirt. Somewhere in the middle it cracked, transitioned. Black racers were resting, nesting in his path. The stones absorbed all day, and even at this hour, they still had not let go of the sun's heat. Pebbles drew the snakes' bellies near. He walked heavy, stomping; the spirals unwound and bolted, their onyx skin caught in the beam-light, then gone. It was strange to see the things themselves after considering their shapes for so long in the hinterlands of narrative.

There were two houses, one on each side of his, and then none for half a mile. To his right was The Family. He had only met them once, the girls loading inflatable tubes into the back of the van, the father saying, "Let's go, let's go," with a vein rising from his forehead. They owned beach property; the father was some sort of park ranger. The ranger reminded the writer of the types of caricature drawings one could get at a theme park. He knew nothing else of them.

To his left was The Witch. He wasn't sure if she worked for the park too, or if somehow remained on what little land the government didn't own. Maybe she was squatting, and everyone was too frightened of her to be bothered. In their few encounters, they never talked about work or land ownership, about their relationships or pasts as anything but abstraction. Her name was Maritza. She called him "Handsome," said to call her "Zaza." He didn't. He had known women like her in Miami, or at least, what he thought he known of them. He had come of age at the end of the eighties when all nerves were electrified with talk of animal sacrifice and daycare cults. He grew up in a culture where anything outside Evangelicalism defaulted to devil worship. Had he been around white people too long, their ideas of morality? Although, weren't his parents progressively unspiritual? They had somehow come of age in their own lives without Catholicism, baptism, saints or spirits.

Maritza resembled those concepts of deviated fellowship he knew: something vaguely holy, Hail Marys and the cross made over hearts. All white attire, sometimes. Saints and spices and herbs and spells. He knew enough of these occultish figures to feel aware, but he didn't think of them that differently, or dangerously. Growing up in a secular family, all things otherworldly were unalluring, equally deceitful. Either all religions were fringe, or none were. Still, there were outliers. Maritza was a point on the furthest X and Y of the plane. She seemed to be one of those people that started off with the congregations and guidebooks before splitting off to unlock a universe of her own. Maritza was the junk drawer of keys in a room with no doors.

Memorial Day—when he had first done this

thing that he did—embarked on his season-long retreat, entered solitude, he talked with Maritza in her driveway, sewing something between them. Although he had conceived of the snake book, he was also trying out a supernatural thriller, trying parapsychology on like a pair of shoes. Why not? Ghosts were the perfect killers: no fingerprints, no barriers.

Maritza was his accidental research, something closer to that world than he was. He had come over for agua fresca three times, at three different times of day. Each visit he mostly frown-smiled, let her do the talking as sweet watermelon seeped into his tongue. The Witch seldom talked about the physical plane, anything connected to the rusted beach chair he sat on beneath her carport. Maritza was a strange woman who invoked in her driveway and lit prayer candles each night. He was both pulled by her and pulled away by a voice that told him not to fuck with her. He sat, sipped, nodded as she raved about subordinate manifestations of the supreme divinity. He didn't like her, but he liked the idea of her. That's why he went back for more sugarwater, to pull from her, from her speech, to imagine her as a guide in his novel, translating the foreign language of death into something he could make palpable for the masses.

He learned it was a mistake to mention ghosts to her in passing, to rip the spirit realm wide open in her presence. He didn't mean to. He tried to be careful around her, sticking to weather, fauna. On his fourth visit, he had grown comfortable with her, had complained of the swamp's mosquitoes mostly,

before his anxiety took over, before he recited a
haunted dream he'd had to her, before his voice
announced, "The house I'm staying in has bad vibes,
it feels like someone was murdered inside." He had
never said "bad vibes" before. It felt right at the time,
when the ghost book was going to happen, when she
was useful.

Later, he caught Maritza grinding a brick on his
doorstep, saw her through a side window sloshing
a bottle of perfumed water against the threshold.
When she left, he cracked open the door, inhaling
lemon and lavender and clove and sea salt. There
were small bones arranged in a circle off to the side.
The sweet, sick smell triggered something. She was
suddenly a human formed in dangerous dimensions.
He knew their little conversations heightened her
affection and communion. He knew this was perhaps
some type of magic shield too, but it went too far.
Blessing or curse, this action was threatening. This
action was no good. He trashed the ghost manuscript
and returned to pathologies, tangible killers with
method work. Even a snake had a body. After that,
after she had done something real, different, become
full and fleshed as The Witch, he spent the summer
avoiding her. She never sought him out after that, so
her invitations were escapable.

Now, here she was, her face glowing purple
under an electric lantern. He needed her night
wisdom. Insects were crackling, stars exploding in
a tiny galaxy of Tesla coils. The zapped bugs added
percussion to her humming, offset by the distant
birdcries. He stood and said nothing, listening to the

noise of nightfall. The Witch was holding a machete, and it was four in the morning, and this was a lesson in self-preservation. On a foldout table were three serpentine bodies in various states of mutilation. They were fat like cottonmouths, but the light was too dim to tell. He imagined infants on a stone, her in a dark robe ceremoniously slicing them. He knew this was Hollywood in his head, ignorance's bubble, hysteria fucking everything over. He knew he should not be scared, should not be prejudiced, that he should not quarantine her, that she was the same as him, yet fear was a muse that pumped life into him. He wobbled the flashlight a little.

"Handsome can't sleep," she said, chuckling as if a joke were told.

He wanted to say something about the machete to feel less powerless, but small talk was an unlearned skill. Acknowledgement saved. The language failed. He wondered if he wrote thrillers because he thought everyone was going to kill him, or if it was the other way around.

"Why are you still awake?" he asked.

"Too many snakes this year. Bad ones. You take the venom and the meat and cast the Devil away. You take the blood for the spirits."

He turned his light off and moved closer to the pale blue hold over the table. The Witch scraped the table with the flat of the blade, blood dripping into a mason jar. A tiny altar was constructed in a corner. There was a statue of a saint he did not know, her face unimpressed, a chalice in one hand, a dagger in the other. At her feet, a bowl of something that looked like sugar, explaining the influx of insects and their death by lightning. He wished he understood the iconographies, the symbols, but likewise felt good in this distance. This proximity to something so impenetrable drew a small apparition of calmness within. The birdvoice burst in scales, scratchy and wooden like a güiro. The Witch turned in its direction, as if noticing it for the first time.

"You haven't been by lately," she said, in a voice neither angry nor hurt. He motioned toward the machete, eyeing the concealing surface, as if to say *Well....* She laughed, hooted. "I am doing the good work! Besides, who could harm that face?" She rubbed the back of her hand against his face. She switched languages in a whisper. He caught fragments that he knew: *guapo, coco, moreno, blanco.* He tried to pick the correct face in response, but she frowned, meaning he selected the wrong one.

"He still don't know Spanish—and from Miami too?" She tsk-tsked, opened her mouth wide in a yawn. He felt embarrassed. He thought about telling her that he was adopted. He thought about making a comment that Spanish and English are equally languages of dominion and erasure, but what did that accomplish? She eyed him, catlike, yawning again, wider. He was surprised at how perfectly aligned her teeth were. He didn't even have dental insurance. Maybe he was too fascinated with the idea of this swamp sorceress. Was he forcing her form into a crone box? Didn't he live alone too? Didn't he tell himself he was different though? Wild Maritza, was she was more? She had to, at least, know more about this ecosystem than he did. The Witch cleaned, wiped her blade, scattered snail shells in a half circle around the saint's foundation. He wondered what he looked like from her eyes. A caterwaul wailed toward them again.

"Do you know what kind of bird that is?" he asked her, remembering his purpose in appearing before her in the middle of the night.

"No, no. Maybe? Could be an egret or an iris. Sounds like it. Sounds like something got it in its jaw. Not all of it though. Not the voice."

One leg locked in a gatormouth, one leg locked in some carnivorous plant's trap—his dream logic returned—him, picturing varied snares and the night bird's flapping madness.

"I can't sleep until I find it," he said, truthfully. She tucked the machete into a paisley fold in her skirt, touched him there with the edge of her fingers.

"We'll find her," she said.

The unrealness of near twilight: he felt a clock moving inside, pictured the disc's hands rotating and rotating. His clockwork body. The night did tricks. Soon, the sun would rise and break, separating the black from the black. For now, his flashlight cast shadows everywhere, the unmovable moving. The Witch hacked at twining diagonals, moved farther in the growth where all things slithered and sank. Webbish things touched his arms, the cusp of his neck. He brushed himself over and over, invisible spiders falling off. This was the Florida he feared the most.

"Move the light over there," she said. He stopped, his feet slowly sticking a half-inch into the muck. She bent, picked a weed-like growth, shoved it in a pocket along her skirt-line.

"What's that for?"

"Protection."

His mind backpedaled, considered that it was he who needed protection. He should have stayed home, finished that chapter. Or slept. The children weren't going to strangle themselves when he was out pushing through humid brush, hunting what exactly, some bird that they might not even reach? Were they even going in the direction of the cry? Was it ludicrous to trust The Witch's judgment as anything other than unsound? What was her own interest in joining him? Was curiosity enough? He wanted to get back to his book, but he couldn't put another word down—or return to his bed—if the bird continued to cry, and the bird did, was.

He thought of all his novels, the failed ghost story, a witch in a tattered corridor, who looked suspiciously like Maritza, hunched with lantern in hand pointing the way. Before him, this one stood straight. He held the failing flashlight. The way it illuminated the dark green was ghastly. He thought of sailing on Biscayne Bay, loading groceries in the trunk of his hybrid car. He thought of all the things that would make this version of himself in the now seem crazed by comparison. He needed to remind himself that he could run back through the brush, lock his doors. Beyond that, he could load his suitcase in his car, retreat home. It could be that simple. But what would that accomplish? His past couldn't block this compulsion he felt in the now. The contrast of himself against himself didn't stop their descent deeper into the landscape.

The bird was no longer a bird but a broken instrument of wood and brass. It was wind pouring through a deflating tube, yet growing louder and louder. He felt himself spiraling in a Fibonacci sequence toward this sound, to this unknowable bird on the other side of sleep. What was this rationale— this rope that tugged him past all the night things that could harm him, kill him with venom, poison, one bite? Black widows and rattlesnakes hid; The Witch discovered.

They came into the clearing, sawgrass surrounding. Black water stretched to a secret endpoint. An upside-down paddleboat touched the shore; crushed beer cans created a mundane sigil in the wet, sloppy earth—and there, where his beam of light hit: a large, white bird nailed to a tree.

Thick metal pinned bone to bark. Its feet did not kick; its body only rose as much as its body allowed. Its long swan-neck curved in a downward V and convulsed, squawking in terror. White droppings and blood painted the tree.

He reached his hand, feeling the air, trying to figure out what to touch first. The bird bent a little and opened its sharp mouth toward him. He retracted.

"Her neck is broken," The Witch said, in a voice both angry and hurt. He moved the flashlight in circles, pointing to all pockets of the growth, as if whatever did this would do them too. The Witch took his wrist with a skinny hand and pointed it at her face. Lit from below, her wrinkles and age showed. Her eyes, oceancold, opened and closed in prayer.

"Do we forgive these people?" she asked. His default thought was still concerned with a killer hiding somewhere near them, waiting to attack with hammer in hand—but he knew who did this was no longer near. The air was light with the smell of beer, and he thought of teenagers, drunk and bored and unaware of their own mortality. Consequences: phantom-like. He had been younger and crueler once. On another timeline, he wondered if it could have been he who caught this wounded creature and pinned its body to the tree. Yet, when he looked at the struggling bird, he knew he never could have done this act.

His arm was hot with sweat; The Witch had not let go. They were conjoined by righteousness. He saw her features, one by one, and knew she was more than some archetype he shaped in his head, more than the herbgatherer, smokeburner, outcast. *Maritza*. Maybe it was the lack of slumber, this peculiar trek into the caliginosity, or his own vanity and ego—but he felt he knew what drove this woman to disappear from others, to stretch a religion with rules of her own, to hide where the only fellowship was with saints and spirits and deities who struck down the wicked. Did he understand who she was? Would he ever see her clearly?

Zaza let go, rummaging in her skirt, his hand

still lighting her ghost-story face. She snapped off a piece of the protective herb with her teeth, recited something. She fed him too, the bitterness curling his tongue in a dark communion. He didn't resist. If this was madness, let madness consume.

"I don't forgive them," he said, in a voice that was almost childlike. He was exhausted and confused and pulled into something he still did not have a word for. Zaza scanned him with her untelling face. He wondered if she had seen him clearly from the start. She pulled his hand away from her, turned toward the unfixable bird and watched it writhe. It looked like a bizarre stagecraft under the spotlight beam. The bird tried to straighten itself in a loop of disjoined thrusts, but nothing worked. It looked at them out of the corner of its bead-eye and closed its mouth—not quite all the way. The only sound in the night was its struggling wheeze.

Mercy, mercy.

And then, with one gesture, it was neckless. The blood filled like a cup at the shoulder's hole, but did not spill over. Its body looked so abstract, attached to a tree like that. He turned the flashlight off, unable to look at it anymore. He could still hear its tremolo call, the notes playing over and over. And then, he only thought he remembered what it sounded like. Maybe that wasn't it. The conclusive quiet from the swamp felt somehow worse than the cries that had filled the hours before. Zaza picked up its beautiful, ophidian neck, wrapping it around her waist like a belt. He didn't know what she was going to do with it, couldn't ask. Protection?

The sky was pinkish-grey. Objects separated from objects, almost looking real again. The sun was rising somewhere, but not here, not yet, the Everglades still preserved in the formaldehyde of sleep. Zaza moved back toward their crushed, hacked path, walking on without him. Had she got what she wanted out of this arrangement? Her body looked tired from its posture, its gait. He wanted words for her magic, but none came. He knew had used her company out of cowardice. She didn't live this deep in the maw out of servitude to him, or any man. Was there a lesson in all this conjuring? Were they now connected in something that no longer needed the conclusiveness of human contact? Or were they more disconnected than ever? Why did he feel an intense need to be akin to her? Had he been scared of her, or scared of feeling like she was more whole than he'd ever be? Maritza felt even more unknowable than before.

He turned, brushing his hand against bark in a space where blood was congealing. He was too afraid to touch the body. He imagined Zaza wrapping that long white thing across her altar, flies summoned over sugar, dead snails, birdneck. Some god was being pacified or beckoned. Some world was being saved or savored in secret. The thing he did, hours bowed before a glowing screen connecting words to words—he suddenly felt small.

The mass of water before him felt more familiar than before, suddenly measurable. This was not the dream or the story of the dream. He pushed the shell of the ownerless boat out into the water, watched it move out of his light and into the muted expanse. Nothing else stirred. No human voice spoke. No water moccasins slid sleek and black over the water toward him. No spiders descended to plunge their fangs in his neck. He was not asleep. Conquered or unconquered. Wild or unwild. What was this land? This body? This tightness in his chest that he wore as a talisman?

He moved from right to left: shoe, sock, shoe, sock, stripping, ensconced in conjury, stepping into the dark. A few aluminum cans rolled down as his foot moved from mud to wetness, their cylindrical forms barely floating, him on his back, joining them, floating too, something new, bedimmed, neither afraid nor unafraid, bracketed to brackish waters.

Their Sons Return Home to Die

A tableau vivant: the sky like toy stuffing, polyester dyed seafoam, like goose down, like loose down, and when the plush clouds open their sons descend down. Their sons come with wings too small for their bodies. The wings are costume, but also attached to skeleton. The bones are part of their bodies. The wings are real too.

The families do not look at the sky when the sons return from the place they went—the place that is here—the place we look down from with our inverted telescopes pointed toward the earth. The families looked the other way when the sons first adorned themselves with wings and ascended. Although the wings were always there.

Like a Sunday paper comic our cumuli are solid sidewalks we walk across. Thousands of feet above our families: this is where we live now. Avenues we cross in long white robes jutting out at our ankles, a gilded sash around our waists matching the halo that hovers above our heads. The halo as a piece of copper attached by wire. It is an ensemble, but it is also sincere. If we look familiar, chalk it up to coincidence.

Their sons are dying. The sons did not choose to die like they did not choose us, like we did not choose each other, although we did—a counterfeit family—one that felt realer than blood. The sons return to their first families, the ones who still inhabit the earth. The sons believe in responsibility. The sons believe they need to go earthbound for their deaths to have meaning. When a son is dying, it is only natural to think of the earth.

If the families looked, just for a moment—up!—they would see scintillation in the darkness, the ultraviolet outline of blacklights. Glow, glow, fog rolling out from fog machines. A discothèque that rivals the sun with its glimmering void. Drops of beer leak from our impossible province in the sky. They could even be mistaken for rain. Their sons descend on a welkin beam, bodies full of sickness, wings aflutter. They return to the place the families inhabit, a clay and muddy place where the only gaze is inward. A place of gravel.

They are sons because they had parents, not because they are young, although some still are. Some have boyish features. Some could even be described as Cupidesque—the round curvature of the face. We are baby-faced if this is how you want to imagine us.

The sons have returned because: pathology. Because: experience. Because suffering. The families do not have wings, never had wings, do not want to gaze upon the careful fan of feathers, two from each shoulder because the body was created in symmetry, the body was created perfect, although it's not.

The families live in a variety of small towns. Small towns are a feature of the earth. Some have one gas station that serves as a general store, sells fried chicken, and that's it. There'll be a post office, maybe a Walmart, but everything else is tree, tree, lake, tree, tree, lake, beating forth across the landscape in a careful rhythm. It is a familiar country, refusing of its own diminutiveness.

Each house of the land holds an oldness to it: the faux-wood panels shooting up and down like a heavenly beam. Linoleum flooring. Formica counters. The sons have returned home to die. The sons ask to call them *Michael* call them *Uriel* call them *Raphael*, but no one does. The parents only want to see their sons as past incarnations, the ones who inhabited the earth before they went skyward. The ones who did not possess wings.

The longer the sons stay, the more the lights dim, the more the houses shift into something funerary. Not funerary. An actual funeral home. Notice the word: *home*, as if a funeral *home* was a permanent dwelling, as if it were a proper place to do anything but yearn. The families wake up one day and their houses are longer, corridors that go to dead ends with red velvet curtains swooping inward. Urns appear, waiting to be filled. Tall bookcases disappear. The books remain at awkward corners until they do not. Glass figurines and paintings, too, go. The house is becoming elemental, becoming a vacated stomach, becoming a place between the past and a future notable for its casualty. A simple carpet, flecked, equally red, replaces all the shag. There are uncomfortable couches and fake lilies in vases. Occasionally, a mock-casket will grow out of the wall, showing off its wares. From somewhere unseen, a church organ plays.

Their sons have good days and bad days. Their rooms have not changed since they first ascended. The rooms stayed the same, dripped in a molasses of age eighteen, maybe younger: the worn-out football poster, the supermodel tear sheet, the concert tickets attached to the headboard of the bed with thumbtacks pushed in deep. Their sons return to a mental space they once inhabited. It is a young space, a teenage space of anything. Their nude bodies in front of the full-length mirror, back facing the silvered surface, head looking over the shoulder to where the feathers began to sprout from skin. Them, seeing the feathers for the first time, feeling cursed, but then feeling blessed, looking for wings everywhere, in everyone. The ingenuity of desire, of looking at a looking glass up close that the enlarged eye is all that can be seen. They practiced kissing the mirror's surface, leaving smudges of lip balm wax behind. Under the sheets they dreamed of a thing. Imagine two doves folded into a shoebox together, the four wings frantically beating into each other. It would be like that.

Their sons tie their wings with childhood shoelaces, with package string; they slip them inside of their bleached robes and sit at the kitchen table, laughing. The families laugh too. It could be like before. They could love each other. They could be the same. They could time travel to when everything was simple, wingless.

The families serve pancakes, stacks as tall as a torso. It's comedic: the giant cube of butter, the way all that syrup slides down. Get it? The food is life, the food is symbol, the food is continuation, but the sons can't keep it down all the same. Corn syrup and corn starch and the starched sleeves of the robe refusing to fold. There's the body getting weak, throwing up an ooze over itself. The discharge. The vomit leaking down the chin. Couldn't the sons make it to the bathroom first? Couldn't they puke in private, with dignity? But they are so weak....

Everything stinks with a pock of nursing home, with a pock of things-to-come. There are facades of stained-glass windows in the long hallways, LED lights behind them pretending to be the sun. No one asks where the windows came from. They feature saints that no one can name.

The sons feel good and go for a bike ride. The sons feel good and go to Wednesday service with their families and read black books in small rooms that also have wood paneling, that also feel antiquarian, feel funerary, feel small. The sons and the parents both sing.

Their sons feel good and miss us, and we miss their sons.

Up here we gallop and mourn. We turn the sound system's knobs up, ugly-cry in the bathrooms here in the vault of heaven. We make cocktails called Obituaries: two parts gin, a quarter absinthe, a quarter vermouth—dry—we dry our wet faces on our sleeves and guffaw through morbidity, dream of descending to the other small towns where we have our own parents, where we are their sons, where we love their sons with a complicated blood.

Their sons get better and worse, better and worse and worse and worse. Pews appear in the garage. Hard chairs emerge softly from the floor, all facing the same direction. The sedan parked in the driveway becomes plumper, longer, taller, resembling a hearse. It is a hearse.

The sons walk through fields of mayapple, ragweed, heal-all, goldenseal, cats ears, bluets, bellwort, bloodroot, trillium, liverleaf, blazing star, verbena, snakeroot, Queen Anne's lace. We play our trumpets, we hark, we send a tiny song through the breeze that reverbs on all the wildflower petals. It is overwrought, but we are overwrought with this sad devotion that throbs through us.

The sons feel good, for a moment, and then: the bed. Death not a noun, but a verb stretching out. Their sons are blue-black, are a yellow-white, are a pink and a red and a green and the opalescent refract of a seashell. Their sons, no matter the color, pale. The familiar sight of cheekbones sinking.

The bound wings flake as aged doilies. They yellow. They rot. Still, they are beautiful to the eyes of us who watch from the empyrean.

The families decide. They sit at the edge of the deathbed with garden shears. They trim. Like a plastic Christmas tree disassembled. Like a hobby, a craft. The blood is not one color. It is dark and thick and leaks like ancient honey. There are horseflies caught in the sweetness. Gnats. They buzz and flap their tiny wings as they fall out of the bonetubes which were once the base of the sons' luscious wings. Wings inside wings inside....

The bone at the base of the shoulder blades is too hard. It can't be trimmed. It looks fake. It looks like someone attached PVC pipe to skin with Sculpey, applied SFX makeup for the blend between avian and human.

Most of the parents cannot gaze at their sons anymore. Most of the parents cannot stand to watch them die like this. But didn't they deserve it? Didn't they tell them not to go? Didn't they tell them not to leave the earth, that if they ascend into the sky, everyone will know they have wings? What will they say if they see you flying? What will they say about us? Even if words like *retribution* and *discipline* cross the parents' minds, no one wants to see a son suffer, not fully.

One of the parents puts an ear up to the bonehole. They expect to hear an ocean. They hear panting. They hear a scream. The son lies quietly, as skeletal as the bone that protrudes out of the son-body. The body: essential. Reduced to anatomy. Meatless. There is no strength in this body, but there are strong noises that come from inside the son. There is a terrible life. It is a voice that is echoed, distorted in a strange way from within. It is louder and bigger than a body. There are snare drums and moans and laughter. It is the laughter of the son. It is certainly his voice, but it is not a laughter any parent has ever heard. It sounds like joy.

The parent puts a parent-eye up against the keyhole of the son. Something ichorous is leaking. Something gilded and fluid and almost possessing a scream or song of its own, even as a liquid. It sticks to the face. The parent-face screams, but still they push on because in this one moment of absolute truth, of relentless curiosity, they can no longer unlook. The parent-eye pushes flush against the bonehole, gazes into the son as if he were a View-Master toy:

It is a blur of arms. It is robes and lipstick and dollar bills. It is a choir, a chandelier, a vinyl sofa where we throne ourselves. The parent looks through a reel, through a glorious portal in the son's body and sees us looking back. Through the malady they don't even have a name for they see us, not as they think we are, but as we actually are. For one fragment between heaven and earth our eyes meet in the dark room of the son's body. Then, the room: obscura, closed, empty, unlit, rayless, gone, gone, gone, gone, gone.

Wherever their son departs to, it is not here. The fake flowers are replaced with real flowers. The parents get their sons' favorite flowers wrong, but we are not there to correct. We can no longer look at this theatre. We seek alleviation. For a moment, we close up the sky. For once, for the burial, for the open casket, we do not look down. We do not want to see what we knew already. We do not want to see this unfamiliar thing that serves their parents, but not us. We do not look down at the corpses of their wingless sons.

We say *their sons*, but they were our sons too. They were our brothers and our brothers and our brothers and we had to pretend to be fathers and we had to pretend to be other-sons and we had to hold each other in this place where we created a new people, a new household, a new home. Yes, a *home*, some idea of permanence. Some idea of inhabiting that cloudy firmament we reside in until we too may have to return home to die. We fear this death that went through them and took them from this place that is here. They were our lovers and our lovers and our lovers and we would turn our backs to salvation in a second to love them again.

We will open up the clouds once more. We will hold this impossible ground in the sky until their parents come out in the fields and stare up. We will meet their scrutiny without our sons in the middle. We will connect somewhere between earth and air. They will acknowledge, and we will nod from the edge of our sky-stage, but we will not descend. We will look down long enough, if only for the angle of our haloes to catch sun. In the flat copper: a tiny refraction of light that looks like the faces of all those who left. The molecules of our sons inside the ashes scattered at sea, their atoms decomposing in wooden boats beneath the earth. We will let the reflection of that star beam down hotly. How fast light moves through the air! If only to blind them for a second! If only so we can be petty, if only so we do not forget! That deciding glare, descending, determining, the harsh light coming down to nick each parent in the eye and remind.

After the End Came the Mall, and the Mall Was Everything

Stud is measuring the customer's thighs. His thighs are as thick as nebuchadnezzars of wine.

"Your thighs are as thick as nebuchadnezzars of wine," Stud says.

"How many liters is that?" the customer asks.

"Fifteen," I say, and the customer nods approvingly. Stud throws the cloth tape with his right hand around the man's back, catches it with his left to measure his expansive chest. This is a familiar parlor trick for those of us who deal with the surveying the human body for a living. Across from Stud's measurings, I wipe down the tuxedo shop's glass cases with Windex—a perfect O of the wrist flick. This is how our game goes: Stud gets mad when I watch him, or when he thinks I'm not working hard enough, so I'm always performing diligence in front of him while judging his allotments quietly from the sidelines. As always, he is being too tight with the tape against the customer's skin. When Stud runs to the backroom to get the correct jacket size, he is certain he got it right.

"What kind of work do you do?" I ask. The man's over-toned muscles say "weight-lifting" say "spandex leotards" say "fighting pits," but you shouldn't let a body say everything about you, so it's always good to ask.

"Dental hygienist," he smiles, letting me see every vaselined tooth under the tuxedo shop's fluorescent lights. Stud returns with a baby blue jacket.

"How does that feel?" Stud asks, pinching at the man's shoulders. "Lift your arms up. Move around. It shouldn't bunch—if it bunches, we may need to go up." He'll need to go up.

Minaudière walks out of the backroom with a cordless drill in her hand, looks at the three of us, making an *Eek* face at me, then immediately ducks back where she came from. Part of my brain wants to follow her into the back, because what was that face? The other half, the half that is moving to my lips, considers *dental hygiene*.

"I've never seen a dentist's office before," I say, curling my lips up to hide my teeth a little. In my head they are all the rotten rock, lunar grey. The customer says, "Ah, well, wish I could give you a recommendation, but I'm not from this part of the mall. I'm visiting from New Mall City. Stopping to visit family before the wedding, and all that."

I'm worried if I ask too many questions, Stud will yell, but usually he behaves in front of the customers, and making small talk is part of the job, so I go for it: "Whose wedding?" I try not to gush over someone from a city part of the mall visiting here in what I cheekily refer to in my head as *the wilderness*.

"I think we need to go up," Stud says. He

needs to go up.

"Middle school friend," the customer says, "The wedding is in Pansy Island Food Court. It looks like an actual island."

"How nice," Stud and I say at the same time in our most retailesque voice. Neither of us have ever been to a food court with a beach, of this I am certain.

When I go into the back to return three pink jackets to their racks, Minaudière is not there. Her favorite shamisen music is blasting from an old boombox we keep on a shelf above the older Singer we hem on. The loud pluck serves its purpose, almost giving a life to all the humanesque suits that watch us always, replacing their silent gazes with song. The bathroom door is cracked open, empty, the light switch off—meaning Mina's not in there either. When I shuffle into the only other possible space left—our smoking closet—I can smell the ghost of something pungent through the other side of the door. When I turn the handle, cracking it a little, a hot cloud of something noxious hits me. "Close the door," Mina mutters past the haze. I step inside, quickly shutting it behind me, and our legs bump slightly. She sighs through her dangling cigarette.

"Sorry," I reply, coughing. One of Mina's hands is on the wireless drill, the other waving smoke in the air, as if beckoning the billows back in, away from the coats and jackets out in the ever-shifting backroom. I stumble to the tiny bench awkwardly, wanting I want to giggle from the excitement of taking a smoking break with Mina, but I know Mina doesn't want me to laugh, so I join her tacitly.

Our smoking closet is about the size of a dressing room, with an old mechanical fan that clicks and whirs, a small glass dome that provides a view to our green sky, that same green sky that is protected by a glass dome of its own. There is something unfamiliar about Mina as she stares me down. Some unfriendliness, someone Stud-esque, someone I don't quite know. But not entirely unusual. She's not always boomboxes and rainbows. She has her moods too.

Mina does this thing, sometimes, where she looks like she's glaring right at you, but you know she's glaring ten, twenty years into the past. Being the oldest of the three of us who work in the tuxedo shop, Mina has more than enough pasts for all our lives combined. Usually she's all laughs and loud cassettes, but sometimes it's like she keeps one eye on a world that no longer exists, and it pulls her back.

Mina and I were both born in the final month of the year. Growing up, my parents said final babies are the closest to death in their birth; they spend their entire lives looking at the past, instead of the future. Mina gives off serious final baby vibes in this moment. She's not even in the same room as me, as little as it is. Our feet have no option but to touch, but still, she's somewhere else. I felt like there was something I wanted to ask her, but now all I can think about is the unsettled look across her face. Sometimes I wonder if I'm the only person in this store who's happy. Well, close to happy. Right?

I wonder what kinds of things make Mina happy. My boyfriend makes me happy, when our feet touch like this, but it's a touch that feels different. Mina is older, her pleasures are more refined, I think.

"Is that a new brand?" I look down at the small white-and-red box in her lap. I don't smoke, so I don't know the specifics. Sometimes I pretend to; I go in the smoking closet and take a five-minute power nap while pretending to light up, because there's some article in our employee handbook that legally allows us smoking breaks. I love the kind of legalities that piss Stud of and protect me. Not that I need the rules to protect me. I have Mina too. She's the one who told me that you have to inhale twice to get it deep down there in your lungs. To get it where it really feels good, calms you down. Once Stud came looking for us, and she showed me how to inhale shallowly, just so the herbal taste hits your tongue and your teeth, but doesn't go down into your lungs. I took the smallest drag, exhaled shallowly when he peeped in to spy on us.

Even without borrowing one of her cigarettes, I can taste this new cigarette. It doesn't taste herbal, but rotten and grey. Mina's usual pack smells like marshmallow, rose petals, honey. This one tastes like suffocation. Mina's eyes refocus on me as I cough slightly.

"It's tobacco," she says, somewhat somber, adding, "Thought you were a farm kid." Her eyes glaze out again. "Has it been that long?" she asks the smoke, which only moves upward, unanswering. A vent beside her has been unscrewed, hanging down by its hinges—she scratches her long acrylics against the slats like a metal güiro—in rhythm to the clicks of the fan. Pulling the cigarette out of her mouth, she billows smoke, holds up the drill to the ring, lets it spin until the air dissolves. I've never seen smoke that dark, that harsh. The harshness enters me, makes me wonder if I should even be sitting here at all. Maybe I should give her space. It'll be soon enough until it's my lunch break, soon enough until I can see Banana again.

"I can go. Stud's going to get mad that I'm not out there," I say, beginning to stand up, but she grabs for my fingers, pulls me back down.

"No. Stud is not the boss," she says, smiling. "And we rarely rest at the same time anymore. So many people have needed formal wear."

"The day just started," I say. She shrugs, bends her head slightly down, to the side. She leans in, brushes my black bangs out from my eyes.

"Just started, but I bet you're already thinking about the food court. You have that young-thing metabolism still. Unquenchable. Insatiable."

Her hand goes down to my chin, maneuvering it from side to side, looking at me like a fresh shipment of inventory. "Your baby fat is disappearing. My little cowboy is growing up. I think I see your very first wrinkle. These—" she says, tapping on the red carton, "They're cowboy *killers*. Toh-back-ee," she accentuates. I know Mina has lived many different lives, been many different people. "I think it died out when I was your age. What did they teach you in school? The wrong things, that's what. I come from a farm family too, like you and your daddy, bet you didn't know that. Ole glamourous Mina. Not a recent family though. A wayback family. Back when there were countries, states, cities. Back when people knew who they were. There's old photos, somewhere. Yellow. Green, like that sky." She looks up. "In that farm country the sky only used to be that green during tornadoes."

"That's like thunder? Or was it water?" I ask, feeling a little bit lost in her past.

"The wrong things, that's what," she says again. She licks her finger, pushes it into the red-hot end of the cig until it sizzles out. "I thought you loved history like your mama. How is your mama? Maybe you're more like your daddy?" Mina frown-smiles. I giggle nervously at her asking about my parents, but also at her using that funny accent.

"Just because the world got tossed up doesn't mean you can't preserve you. You should know these things. You used to come from somewhere. We all did. Not everyone had long family trees, but some did. Now no one does. There were countries, and then there wasn't. Then there was nothing that was not the mall. Some people like this, but I'll tell you it's a nightmare, it's a nightmare to not understand where you come from, to not know yourself truly."

I stare at her, smiling. She sighs. "I don't know if this is getting through to you. This isn't just another one of my Mina stories. I know you love my mall stories. Old malls, old Minas. These cigarettes take me there, to that old world, the one you never saw. Tobacco is gone, but you can still buy these, if you know where to find them," Mina says, tapping the pack, "but they're expensive. They kill you quicker. It's not the same when the crop is long done. Got to save them for days when I want to feel the death in me move a little faster. Wistfulness. You know what that word means?" I shake my head.

She puts the half-smoked stick back in the pack, slips it into the vent, replacing the grate. I go to ask why she's hiding them, but then I see Stud's face in my mind, and stop myself. In seconds she's managed to drill the vent back up, hiding those killers of cowboys. As we leave the tiny room I wonder what cowboys did, why I'm a little one. Most of all—why did they need to be killed?

"Lift your arms out like a *T*," Mina says. "No!" she cackles. "Like the capital letter, not a *tea*pot." She sprays me with Febreze as I straighten my arm from its handle and spout, then mists herself, before disappearing into the dark aisles of the jackets with her drill. I wonder why she tries to get rid of the smell. So it won't get on our merch? Or is there another reason? She hums, walking away from me, down the dark, endless aisles of the backroom. Although I can no longer see her, I can hear her building some new shelving unit: the never-ending whir of the drill.

When I return to the floor, Stud immediately shifts into sly interrogation. "Where were you?" he asks. "Bathroom," I reply. I want to shout, "I was taking a smoking break with TO-BACK-EE!" or even say something defensive like, "You looked like you were handling the customer fine," (even though he got the measurement wrong), but it's easiest just to pretend I was peeing. Even though he's worked here much longer than me, Stud doesn't understand this store, just like he doesn't understand how to measure bodies, just like he doesn't understand me. He always has to go to our backroom at least once per customer, grabbing something slightly larger, slightly smaller. I've never once criticized him though, mostly because I'm scared of him. Usually Mina will sass him on my behalf, or at least pretend to, and I just act quiet and dumb and let it happen. I shouldn't be super rude about Stud though, because it's not like I'm perfect at retail either. I have my weaknesses too.

I've been thinking about these kinds of things more these days, wondering how everyone else sees me. Mina says I'm at that point in my life where I know everything, and I'm going to have to spend the rest of my time on this planet unlearning. I think I get that. Although I think it's a rite of passage to get to an age where you can complain about teenagers. Mina is definitely at that age. She's probably as old as Stud and me combined. Stud complains about everything in general, whether he's earned it or not, so his age doesn't really count.

My mind wanders for a second as I linger in the doorway between the storefront and the background, and when my thoughts returns, Stud is so much closer, sniffing the collar of my button-up. He gets that look on his face like he always does before he says something mean—there's a certainty in the eyebrows and corner of the mouth. He's sussing me

out, even though I'm legally alloed a smoking break!
The nerve! I cut him off before even one syllable can
enter the air: "How old do you think Mina is?" I ask.
It's the first random thought that pops into my head.
Whatever it was he was going to say went elsewhere.
Stud has been disarmed. I can tell he's trying to re-
track his thoughts, trying to get back to the barbs he
had for me, when a customer begins to walk through
the door carrying a garment bag to return a rental.
"I've got this," I say, ducking down, running away
from Stud's watchful gaze.

For a while the bodies come through the door
like this: not new customers but those returning the
suits hung by their hangers in the shiny, dark bag
with the equally shiny shoes weighing them down at
the bottom. I always like the new customers the best,
making small chat while we talk about their dreams.
There's something somewhat melancholic about
the end of the transaction—the special event—the
wedding, the funeral, the prom, the dance—being
over. Sometimes people I spent an hour talking to
just thrust the bag toward me and nod. In those
moments, these people that felt like acquaintances
become less. After a while they all feel the same:
strangers who increase my pile of work, all these
parts I will have to disassemble and hang up in our
storage space where we are always running out of
room.

We have to be vigilant, use our space well, or
else it could mutate overnight. That's the unofficial
motto of the store, or else, the world. It's why Mina is

constantly somewhere between building new shelves and preparing for another inventory binge. That's why the drill is practically a cyborg extension of her hand. Bolting metal to metal, dragging old inventory out from the shifting shelves, preparing for new deliveries. There's corporate policy, of course, but we don't think corporate really knows how zoetic our backroom is. It's defined by nearly endless shelves moving into darkness, overhead ducts, blasting cold air; they cause the sleeves of the tuxedos to move like dancers. We're supposed to get new coats in tomorrow, new dancers, although Stud said some mall paths changed near foreclosed stores and our mail is all messed up again. That's how it always is. Pathways inside pathways. But good business keeps things stable. Capitalism is complicated like this, but at least it keeps us safe from the mall's distortions.

When I'm done putting rentals away in the background, I head out front again. Stud has disappeared to do something—probably lost in a separate corridor of our storage space—so I lean against a fitting mirror (even though we're not supposed to lean). Stud has that kind of strut, that kind of conviction where even if I'm not sure he's actually busy, his attitude sells it. I wish I could be that sure, display myself that way. The thing is though, I can see Mina and Stud doing this for the rest of their lives, I guess. This is temporary for me. But even if that's true, I have to be committed to working hard, doing my job well.

When it becomes apparent that neither Mina nor Stud are emerging from the backroom any time soon—that lovely quiet from the lack of coworkers and customers and voices from mall passersby—I stand behind the cash register and stare out into the long hallway of the mall. There are those moments in retail where the second hand drags on. I think about my boyfriend, Banana, the most in these moments. How happy I'll be to see him later today. I daydream, eyes blurring with the neon lights of the Brookstone across from our store. Occasionally a costumer will walk inside to test out a massage chair for free. My eyes unblur, focus again, when something orange catches my attention.

Between our two businesses, a fox spirit sits on a mall bench, licking its paw like a common housecat. I try to count its tails, but it wags them. Twitch. Seven. Nine? There is a translucency to its fur, and when it dives off the wood it does not stop on the tile floor, but slides through, goes somewhere impenetrable to me. These types of creatures annoy me; these beings of magic stepping over the line, leaving their world to bother ours. Before my mother moved away to take a university job in Shoppingumooru, she gave me an ancient book of Japanese folklore, said it was passed down in her family for generations. I can't read it, but I love the illustrated plates, especially the one of kitsune, who looks just like the spirit I just saw. This is only the third or fourth time I've seen a fox spirit. Mom says we get visited by our pasts, our ancestors. But now the trickster spirit is gone. It didn't even try to speak to me, unlike the previous times. Perhaps it just wanted to make itself known, to remind me of something. Family? My eyes soft focus and blur in the spot where the orange vulpine body previously sat, and I wonder when I'll see Mom again.

The warm feeling of family is interrupted by a sharp finger under my ribs. I screech. I'm re-centered in my body, back to witness the nasty face of Stud, who carries his unhappiness at the corner of his nose. Twitch.

"Instead of standing around zoning out, why don't you help Mina in the back? She needs help finishing those shelves."

I don't mind assisting Mina—that's not it—I just don't believe him. He knows what I see when I'm alone—what things announce themselves to me. He's too old, and he certainly has never seen any fox spirits. This is why I bet he secretly wants to trade places with me. He wants to stare out into the mall and see what I see.

I find her by the music. Mina's mini-boom is suspended from a clothes hanger nearby. I sway to the plucks, the assistant-at-ready. I'm the one who got Mina into this music, these songs that came from my childhood. My parents come from the part of that mall that was called Japan—when it was called that. My mother has a soft spot for antiquity. She collects old things. She told me no one plays the shamisen anymore, but she's been trying to find me one, saying I could probably figure it out for myself. I think this is what Mina means when she talks about the past, talks about a selfhood that isn't just defined by life inside the mall. Music: it came from places. There were regions, identities, and this music is supposed to be part of me.

I lean into the sound, my hands gripping down on giant screws for Mina's shelves. The crosshairs on the screw's heads are equally wide and deep. I stick my fingertips inside them and they ride on my fingers like the long claws of a wilderness witch. "I vant to send vu on a kwwwest," I say in an accent I am uncertain of, flexing the nails in a gross, sexy way. There's too much movement and three of the screws pop off and roll under the hanging coats. Mina stops the power drill and sighs.

"Joshua, what did we say about wearing screws like finger puppets?" Her tone has gone from a world-weary older sister to an annoyed mother.

"You also said we can have fun back here!" As her tone gets older, I get younger.

I'm already on the floor, although it's dark and dusty with all the loose hairs of coat thread. Mina is continuing to talk to me, but her Min'yo folk music is so loud. Part of me is trying to find the screws, listen to Mina's drowned out words, and comprehend the lyrics of the loud shouting between all the plucks all at the same time. I collect the screws and count them and stand proper this time. My elbows tucked into my ribs. My hands jut out like an offering, like my hands are a water bowl for birds to drink from. I hold the oversized screws waiting for Mina to take them as the shelf continues to grow.

"You've felt really different today—distant," I think aloud to Mina, and then feel an immediate half-regret at my words. It's not that Mina is ever cruel or judgmental, it's just that I respect her kindness. I don't want my thoughts to be wrong, for her to see me differently based on my observations.

"That client you had this morning? I knew him," she smiled over her shoulder at me, reaching down to take a screw.

"That old white guy going to a beach wedding?"

At this, Mina cackles. "I'm old too, Joshua. He looked different. I looked different."

Despite what she says, Mina dresses young, wears cool, aqua lipstick that glows against her skin. She styles herself better than most of the people my age.

"Did something bad happen between you two? Is that why you were hiding?"

She looks over her shoulder again, stops the drill, slings it to the side. "Why do you have to be so nosy?" she asks in a mock-harsh voice. She extends a nail to bring pause to the music. It's quiet as we listen to the whir of the ancient A/C breathe between us. She whispers, "We knew each other briefly, but it was more of a one-night stand situation. You'll get it when you're older. Sometimes it's easier just to hide in the backroom. Sometimes it's better."

I'm giddy with all the information I'm getting. The low tone of her voice tickles something inside my ear that goes down to my heart. I love Minaudière because she's seen it all, because her age has been hidden. She's lived all over the mall—in quadrants like New Mall City. She's flown in airplanes from one part of the mall to all the territories I've never seen. Shoppingumooru. The Mall of India. Antarcticmall. Stud once told me she was a CEO of some company

in the mall that went under, but swore me to never ask
her about it. She makes me want to go somewhere,
live a different life, leave this part of the mall I was
born in. I feel my heart swaying again.

"When was this?" I ask.

"Before I ever lived in this part of the mall,
that's for sure."

"Where?"

"Where did I live at the time, or where did we
fuck?"

I gasp. I hadn't even considered the latter, and
how Mina is smiling a wide smile. Now she's neither
a sister or a mother, but a distant friend coming
back to overshare, to unpeel some sordid secrets
of the world still unknown to me. She cannot hide
her delight; she wants to throw me a freebie, tell me
something that will shock me.

"In a drained fountain in some foreclosed alley
near a dead mall," she blurts out.

"No," I gasp again, face flush. I don't know if
she's telling stories or not, but I can't imagine Mina
lying. "There were old quarters left on that tile. I
stuck some of those children's wishes up in his coin
slot and he *loved* it." I can't stop myself from putting
my hands over my mouth, screaming.

"What are you schnooks doing back here?"
Stud barges in with his baritone voice, annoyed at
our hollering. He's always countertenor with the
customers, reserves this harsh lowness for us. Stud
thinks he's the manager, but he isn't. Minaudière
would never throw her authority around like that
though, so she lets him play out his power fantasies.

"It's a secret between us girls," Mina smirks. Stud rolls his eyes. "OK, *ladies*, then I'm taking my lunch, and that means Joshua needs to be up front, because the floor must not be unatten—" Mina has already popped the screw drill-bit back into the play button of the boom, followed by the spin. Stud's voice is drowned out as I slink past him, prepared to man the store alone.

When I am dusting our jade cufflinks, my mind is off somewhere, thinking of sex. It's not that I haven't imagined sex with Banana, but I guess I've just never thought about what it could entail. Usually, when I think of us, it's this abstract thought of our bodies, erect, touching. Inside, outside, skin. My mind starts dreaming of an apartment in New Mall City, just Banana and me, sprawled naked on a bed with red, silk sheets. Wherever my fantasies were going, they run away fast: a purple-haired crone creaks into the store, her hands like ancient corkscrews rested against the glass countertop.

I watch the spot I just wiped down, wonder if there's any oil left in the crone's fingertips to leave prints behind. A spherical red hat on her head bobs like a cherry as she points. She looks like one of those plastic cupcakes they set out on dessert trays at restaurants. "Those are nice cufflinks," she rasps out. "Would you trade them for this comb?" There is suddenly a wooden comb between her fingers. When her fingers brush against the prongs I am reminded of the shamisen, and then, too, I think of an old forest, although I've never been in one. I wouldn't know. The farm I grew up on was small, exact, with calculated rows of crops in an insular space. "When this comb is thrown to the ground, it will sprout into a thousand-acre wood," she says.

"No," I say, "We only take legal tender."

"Child…" the cupcake crone continues, but I cut her off, "No. Your kind isn't even supposed to be here. Why does your kind keep bothering me?" I say this more to the store than to her.

There is something glittering in her eyes; an answer.

"I'll call the mall police," I say, hovering my hand over the store phone. I'm not sure my threats mean anything, or if she even knows what the mall police are, but somehow, it works. She collapses on the floor, dissipating into a puddle of red burlap.

"You know, old shawls don't clean up themselves," I speak again to the empty air and move toward the dustpan we keep beneath the cash register.

I know there was a time before the mall enclosed our planet, a time when malls only made up a small portion of the planet, instead of all of it. I know there were forests and oceans and beaches and skyscrapers outside the mall, but now there is nothing that is not mall. I've spent my entire life being issued warnings: warnings about the dead parts of the mall where other creatures live, where beings with powers beyond humanity take you away, gobble you up. They say: buy. They say: build. They say spend your money, grow your businesses, live your life or the magic will devour you.

They told us in school that it's not uncommon for more benevolent creatures to wander through our places of business, but that still, you can't trust them. Even if there's a thing as good magic, it leads to bad magic. Once they take over our spaces, creatures like the nightdogs wander through—who only seek blood. That's why you have to say *no* when they offer you presents, or quests, or adventures. It's said if you go on a quest, you probably won't come back. No one ever talks about these things in detail though, although everyone is aware of them. One week of sex ed, one week of magic ed. Abstain, abstain. It's like that. It's never enough. We just have to remain vigilant, and fearful, and not ask too many questions. It's like this collective secret that everyone knows about, but no one ever has any answers for. I guess that's because everyone's supposed to hit a sort of second puberty, where you grow into capitalism, and it protects you. You have to believe that commerce will save you. I know in magic ed class they said most people stop being offered quests by the time they're twenty years old. I wonder if it's normal to be approached as often as I'm approached. I wonder when this will all go away. It stresses me out, these unknowable things slinking toward me, speaking, making offers again and again.

In the mall, I am always fending off donors and oracles and gossiping animals who try to send me on some enchanted errand. In the mall, I am just trying to work my 9-to-5, trying to pay my mall bills and wait for my mall lunch that I'll eat with my mall boyfriend: my mall boyfriend who I'll move in with once we have enough money saved. Banana and I have talked about moving away together to a different mall city—even a different mall quadrant—since we were sixteen. I could be mature, could be like Mina who has known many men, many lives. Sometimes I think she gives me these glimpses into her adulthood because she wants me to grow up faster, join her there. Maybe it's the opposite. During these hours I'm slowly trying to get to known Mina better, and get to know Stud less—but it's like the more time I spend with Mina, the less I know her. Stud, he's as transparent as ever. He spends the day on the same schedule, flowing through the same sour moods. All these thoughts of magical journeys combined with managing Stud's temperament dampens my mood.

I think about the weird crone again. A thousand-acre wood? Surely that can't be real, but I've heard about magic, how it could destroy our stores, just like that, if you let it in. A small part of me wonders what it would mean to accept a quest, take a magic object, do these inhuman people— these creatures—a favor. I think about our store, my coworkers, the vulnerability of all of us, until all I can think of is the hollowness of my stomach. I pat it softly, whisper, "*Soon.*"

Stud always takes the first lunch. I know he doesn't eat breakfast, which is why he always gets hungry so fast, and also why I suspect he's always so cranky and pale. I always eat second, always eat with Banana, who brings me a new bento box each day. It's this precise time of day: when I'm alone, when

Mina is managing the back, and Stud is at lunch, and I am just with myself on the floor, that I always feel much more susceptible to wandering archetypes.

There are times of the year when there are no homecomings or proms, no winter formals, or summer weddings, or many weddings at all for that matter. One of our busiest seasons just ended, meaning this is one of those times. It's when the hours stretch. It's when less people walk by. It's when I make sure all the coats we have on display share an equidistant negative space between them on their racks. When I polish and sweep and re-hang each pair of pants until there is something sinisterly sanitized inside the store. Every stray mote of dust becomes punished. This makes me feel neurotic and bored, but also important.

"Say," a voice whispers into the quiet with its sibilance, "Do you know the Department Farm a few miles away?" I turn to see a blue hare stretching across our tired leather chair. It's a chair usually reserved for bored family and lovers, friends who will not be fitted in tuxedos. The hare rolls from its back to its stomach, letting its long legs dangle over the side of the arm. As it moves its hair gets refracted in the light, not quite fur but fibers like all the scales of a rainbow trout. I can't believe another one has come in here!

"The Belk Farm or the Sears Farm?" I ask, annoyed, pushing the Swiffer hard into the already squeaking tile. I'll reluctantly engage.

"Sears," the rabbit hisses back.

"Yeah," I say, "I spent the first few years of my

life on that farm. My father worked on that farm."

"The farm is in great danger," the blue hare whispers in a whisper that is not a whisper, "A blight, a nightly poison will ruin the land. Only you can stop the sowing of the salt," each s escaping its mouth like stale breath slipping out of an air mattress.

"That can't be true," I sigh, moving closer to the hare.

"It's true," the hare says, matter-of-factly, and lets its long incisors of its still-open mouth press lightly into the leather arm.

"I guess I'll have to join the Belk CSA then."

"No—" the hare says, "—Yes," I cut in. "Don't you see I have a job to do, Hare. I can't go on a quest for you. I have to be here to rent tuxedos to all the people who need tuxedos in their lives. I have to be there for their celebrations." I grab the hare by its scruff and hoist it up. "I have to be here for their joy and their homecomings and their graduations," I add.

"A cursssse," the hare begins.

"No curses. You aren't even supposed to be in here. I'm not even supposed to talk to you. You're going to ruin everything!" I find myself nearly screaming.

"B-but," the hare stutters.

"No," I say again. "And who are you to have the authority to send me on a quest, or punish me for not going? As if my hourly wage wasn't bad enough…!" I walk out into the nearly empty mall. I set the hare on top of one of the giant ceramic planters with bromeliad bursting toward the skylight.

"Fine," the hare says, as I start to walk back toward the store. When I turn to look over my shoulder, it's gone. I think about the farm I grew up on—a knot in my stomach—but then a hotness in my face, thinking about the hare, its quest, its lies. When I turn back to the tuxedo shop, Stud is a foot away from me, a French fry dangling flaccidly from his lips. He slurps it up like a worm.

"The front of the store should never be unmanned," he says, pointing at the empty shop.

"Hey!" I say. "There was—"

"There are rules, Joshua. Someone could have stolen something because you stepped outside of our store."

"There's no one even around."

"There are rules. If someone steals something, the person who left the store unattended will be fired." Stud says this all with a sobriety, although he moonwalks back into the store. There is a playfulness to his cruelty. He walks backward so we can retain eye contact, so we both know he was back in the store before me, for those brief few seconds the floor was technically unattended.

"Oh Minaaa," he sings as he lifts the old landline, begins to dial what I imagine is our corporate office. I've only been here six months, but Mina's told me stories. How draconian Stud gets, tattles on the newbies to get them fired. She compared this to the way that cats play with mice they catch. A game, a tease, until the viscera pours out the belly. Harmless until the harm is done. She says he's jealous of me because I'm young and fun, which, if I think about it, is the same reason she probably likes me.

When Minaudière comes through the curtains onto the floor she doesn't even duck. Her blonde updo bops into the top of the doorframe. She must know this song. "Put that phone down—now. If you throw anyone else under the bus you're going to need a mechanic." Stud hovers the earpiece a little lower from his ear. "Now," she says, again, and he hangs up the phone. It's too much, though. I can't deal with Stud's antagonism today, even if it's in jest. I duck past Mina, my head low, into the back, where all the colorful coats look down at me like all the ancestors I've all but imagined.

Mina knocks at the bathroom door. I know it's her because I can hear the way she hits the door with her acrylics. Stud would use his curled fist. I'm wiping my puffed eyes with toilet paper.

"Joshua," she says in a kind voice.

I say nothing in response.

"Jo-shu-a Jinn-ou-chi," she sings my name as a radio jingle, each syllable climbing in octave.

"I don't want to get fired," I cry out through the door.

"No one is getting fired," Mina says. I heard her whispering to Stud, but can't make it out.

"Can Stud get fired," I cry out again.

"Hey!" Stud says.

"A-hem," Mina says.

"I'm sorry," Stud apologizes. He knocks on the door with a curled fist. "I was only teasing."

"WHERE IS EVERYONE?" I hear the familiar voice of Banana shouting, his voice distant, as if coming from a rollercoaster on its downward swoop while I wait for him on the ground.

* * *

Banana and I always sit in the same corner booth of the Victrola Crown Food Court. It is the Food Court most equidistant to where both of us work. It has a vinyl covering that puffs out with patterns of cute, smiling cats.

"Are you sure you don't want anything savory?" Banana asks. We sit with a parfait glass between us; it is whipped into an upward spiral with kiwi and mango syrups and a cherry like a crone's hat.

"No," I sulk, before remembering that I forgot. How could I forget! "Oh, I mean, yes! The bento!"

Banana smiles, takes a lemon-shaped bento box out of his bag, cracks it open on our shared table. In the bento is a portrait of us, our two faces painted as profiles in rice. My dark green hair—nori; Banana's yellow hair—delicious bell peppers. Our lips kiss in akami.

"This is so sweet," I blush. Banana makes me a bento box every day. Careful dinosaurs constructed out of arugula and carrots. Hello Kitty with a hot dog for a hair bow. Mickey's cartoon face: an expertly sliced mask of provolone. I try to bake Banana sweets, but all I ever manage to get right is the same chocolate chip cookies again and again, which is surprising, because I've failed at simpler tasks. One summer when my CSA had white Shimizu peaches, I tried to make Banana a jelly and accidentally scorched it. I sigh in remembrance, taking some cookies out of my bag. I break one in half and use the plastic baggie as a plate. "Thank you," Banana says.

Banana works at a kitchen store with intermalltional cooking supplies. Bento boxes, of course, but also aebleskiver pans, chapatti presses from the Mall of India, comal for tortilla, and camping cutlery kits for all of those who bravely explore the wilderness. There are still so many wildernesses.

Banana feeds me a spoonful of cream, keeps putting a napkin beneath both my eyes, although I'm certain they're dry. "So besides Stud being meshugenah, how else has your Monday been?"

"Okay," I say. "A muscleman came in, and Mina said she fucked him in another life."

"Oh," Banana says. His face is unrevealing, but I know he shies away from these topics.

"She says she fucked him in a dead mall's fountain."

Banana's eyes widen a little. Whenever Banana feels a little nervous, or like the topic we're about to discuss is not proper for others' ears, he code switches and we talk to each other in Japanese. He speaks it better than me, but it's easy to catch up. It's easy to speak something, even if you can't write it well. "It makes for a good story," says Banana, "but not for good practice. Do you think she was telling the truth?"

"I think she always tells the truth, but I also think she says outrageous things to entertain me, and maybe herself too."

Banana nods, then leans in a little, puts his face against my hair. It feels so tender, his hot breath going through the strands. Then, Banana pulls back, clenches his nose.

"What's that smell on you?" he asks.

"Oh! Mina also smoked this type of cigarette I'd never seen before in our smoking closet. Is that it?"

"Tobacco?" Banana says.

"Yes!" I reply. "How did you know?"

"You've never heard of tobacco, Joshua?" Banana looks at me appraisingly.

"I dunno—should I have if it's not a thing that's made anymore? Mina was harshing on me, says they didn't teach me the right things in school. I also felt embarrassed because I couldn't remember what type of weather a tornado was."

Banana half-shrugs, "Weather is for outside, and there's no outside anymore. Old people are always rambling on about the things that only they remember. It makes them feel important when they get to leave us out. Still, you should have paid more attention in school. You were always sneaking your headphones up through your long-sleeved shirts, listening to music in class." Banana kisses the back of my hand and laughs. I know this is the part of my personality that he likes.

It's true that I never paid much attention in school. I didn't *dislike* school per-say. I didn't like writing or reading or math or physical education or science or art class, but I liked music and lunch. I loved history class more than anything: all those factoids of a world that's gone. Maybe that's why I adore Mina's nostalgic ramblings, because I want to be part of that past too. Us, the final babies. I want to know all the yesteryears. I love vintage clothes and old rituals. I love cookbooks that detail ingredients that no longer exist. I love to remember the stories of all that will be forgotten. It helps me think of a better future.

Before my mom went back to school, got her graduate degree, and took a job teaching history at the University of Shoppingumooru—leaving me alone with Dad—she was here all the time. She filled my head with all these ideas of the past: how magical it can be. My mom has an enduring love for our world before it ended. Those are the stories she told me, the ones I feel connected to. A past, a family, a lineage, a world. A real world.

I wrote many five-paragraph essays in school on these old versions of our planet before it re-wrote itself. I re-wrote the same essays year after year—so much that all that all mall intel and apocrypha is ingrained within me. I think of Mom's stories all the time, the ones that go: there was a time when leaving a mall (which people only temporarily visited to shop), you went through a department store, and exited into a parking lot, where you had temporarily left your car. There was an outside world you returned to. Now, when you exit the department store, you're in another mall. Nothing is not mall. There is no outside. Everything is mall, and its interiors always shift and change. This is why we install new shelves, constantly stock new products. The activeness of our store keeps it static, away from the whims of the living mall which grows like moss, magically mutates its insides. For the mall to be living, it also has to be dead. If you go too far into dead parts of the mall, you might not come back. Dead malls connect to other dead malls and suddenly you are in a void of uninhabited space. The dead parts are filled with the most extreme kinds of magic: the kind that can devour you whole. They say children and teenagers are the closest to magic, the most vulnerable, and that's why we are preyed upon, why we must be the wariest.

Do people outside of my family secretly obsess over these stories as much as we do? They say mall spelunking is dangerous, but I dream of it, dream of those horrifying spaces, like Mina's story from earlier this morning. To have sex near a dead mall!

Banana taps his hand on my knee, and I'm pulled from these dreamy remembrances of my mother's stories to Mina's stories to the place that I now sit, connected by the touch of the one I love. I feel giddy with all of these histories inside me.

"I think it could be fun to recreate Mina's dead mall fountain adventure," I say, sticking my tongue outside my mouth, licking a bit of cream off my fingernail. I saw this in an R-rated movie at the AMC theater my family lives above.

"Joshua!"

"What," I say, "I think it's time." I rub my

hand across the whiskers of the booth, the tiny feline heads. Banana removes his hand from my knee.

"Maybe when we move in…" Banana pauses, "…together." He finishes his sentence and pauses before he starts back up. "High school is over and we're certainly too old for sleepovers."

"I'm just tired of being a virgin."

"Well, I'm not sneaking out after dark to fornicate with you in a dead mall. We'll be eaten by a moon ghoul, or else the nightdogs will devour our bones."

"I'm not scared of the nightdogs and they don't *always* eat bones," I say, although we both know that's not true.

When you grow up somewhere, the more time you spend there, the less judicious you are on how safe a place is or isn't. You *know*, but you forget. The part of town we live in, while not run down, is underpopulated compared to other parts of the mall. People refer to this part of the mall as *the country*, although this annoys me. We have some very upscale shops that opened up recently! The more expensive a shop, the less magic can enter it, supposedly. Although less people in general means that magic gets curious—or brave.

Even in my conflicted protectiveness of my stomping grounds, I am ready to leave my job, my life. I love Dad, but I'm tired of living with him. It would be nice to rent a place out with somebody who doesn't snore. I think about making big moves, life changes, going on adventures. My thoughts turn to quests and dead malls again. When Banana says *nightdogs* I think of all the less pleasant creatures, the ones who don't make bargains as much as take them. When I think about all those quests I've been offered lately, I shudder a little. It's thoughts like these that make me feel like it's acceptable to stay inside my comfortable, safe life.

I think about telling Banana about the hare and the crone, but I know he'd just tell me to ignore them or call the police. I'm sure they'd just vanish by the time the police would arrive, even if I did call. I think about the magic of their world and a sourness curls on my tongue. I think of their parts of the mall, their abandoned routes that link to the dead malls they reside in: all the foreclosed stores and broken glass lining their horrible alleys. These places are uninhabited, but also, inhabited—where everything is either quiet, or wild, or haunted. Supposedly, there's a nearby colony of nightdogs who roam after the stores close. I saw it on the news. Everyone always talks about them, in whispers, as if they are the worst of the local magic we're hounded by. There's been remnants: the bones that cannot be eaten, or don't need to be. The mall police have their methods, supposedly. You can call them, but it seems like they barely do anything half the time. There's always gossip about people being fed to moon ghouls, to cats as big as motorcycles, to wilderness witches, to all those nightdogs who lurk the perimeters of our part of the mall. This is why everyone is always trying to drum up business. Perhaps because the mall police can't arrest nightdogs. Maybe there's no mall laws against magical feral dogs. Maybe magical feral dogs have just as much rights as humans do, even if they can turn their flesh into shadow. My thoughts spiral toward a dizzying darkness as I continue to shove food into my mouth.

The umami pleasure of fatty meat against my tongue isn't doing much to the fast heartbeat inside my chest. Having thoroughly freaked myself out, I go to put my hand on Banana's knee. His face grows serious, puts his hand over mine, moves it to the vinyl seating. "Joshua... my dad has been sick again," Banana says. I was smirking because I thought he was going to scold me for not paying attention, for getting lost in my imagination again. But here is my face, dropping.

"I may need to quit my job soon and go work at our family's store," he adds. "Less money, y'know?" Banana fingers a single piece of rice that has fallen onto the table. There's a lot of implications to this, all the things this could mean. I want to *say what about our dream*, but it's cheesy and high school is over and I'm trying to be more adult about everything.

"We're supposed to get a big shipment tomorrow," I say. "All sorts of coats and accessories. Maybe I can get you something, something the color of a daisy."

Banana is quiet, until he smiles, says, "or a #2 pencil."

I move my hand back on Banana's knee, and this time he does not move it away. When we kiss our lips are the exact same size, it feels odd how they push into each other. People have said before we look like brothers, and I'm not sure if that's just people being gross or if it's true, but I don't want to think about Banana as a twin. For a second though, it does feel like I'm kissing a sheet of glass, a mirror. Like there's only one of us. Like I am kissing something flat, something that will be gone soon. When our lips pull apart, I feel a drop, like a subtle distance is introduced. Not aloneness anymore, but like we're two people, like we were always two very different people. I want Banana to be happy, but I also want so many other things.

"I think business hasn't been great at the store," I say. "I think our backroom was acting up again—shifting, changing. I'm seeing more and more weird creatures and magical things." I pause, watch Banana's face, the one I expect. "They keep asking me to go on quests," I add.

"Just ignore them," Banana says. "They'll stop bothering you soon. There's too many people around during the day for any of them to cause real mischief. They only have real power when you're alone with them. You could always call the mall police too," Banana adds. He seems somewhat disinterested or uncomfortable or skeptical.

"I know, I know," I say, slightly annoyed.

"If you're feeling bothered by...these things... it's probably safer to take a vacation," Banana says, looking down at his lap. Vacation? Who said anything about a vacation? It sounds like a non-sequitur, but of course it's not. "There's nothing stopping you," he says, looking up. "These...things are more prevalent in the country. You've always talked about the city. You could move to the city."

Just me? What is he trying to say? What about my dreams, Banana's dreams, our dreams?

We both take turns opening our mouths to say something, but nothing comes out. We turn these unformed words into breaths. I imagine we'd look like a silent film of goldfish from afar. We take turns eating scoops of the bento and parfait until all that's left is our shared tuna flesh lips in the plastic lemon, a cherry at the bottom of the creamy glass.

When I lean in to give my goodbye kiss, Banana sneezes, and as he turns my mouth slides down the side of his face, resting somewhere near the back of his neck, where the hair there smells so new, so clean, so nameless, and I feel disoriented, like I'm meeting him for the first time.

* * *

I pass a vintage shop on my walk back to work, see a fur coat in a window that reminds me of one I have in my closet at home. I love fur coats from animals that no longer exist—the kind I read about in folklore, legends, myths. Foxes. Sable. Hare. Tanuki, like the one from Mom's book. These tales give me a voice to speak through. I always think of these stories when I go on my walks about the mall—walking to work, walking to and from my lunch break. I zone out, recede into my little bubble, the faces of strangers blur out as I become only the balls of my feet bouncing from tile to tile, only my stride and the history I feel around me, passing through me.

My storybooks go: it's said that unseen natural
forces got fed up, possessed the artificial. It's said
ancient spirits rose up from crevices of the earth and
turned the industrial into the organic. It's said that
strip malls grew like kudzu, that scrap metal and
plaster consumed gas stations, grocery stores. That
all buildings became one building and that building
was our world and that world was a mall. An old
fog, too, it came from the bottom of the oceans and
made people dizzy, forgetful. Time moved differently.
That ancient creatures appeared and challenged us,
asked us to serve them, to do them favors, to co-
exist, or else, surrender. It's said there was brief war.
It's said there was a long war. It's said that everyone
forgot how long the war was. It's said so much of the
land and the buildings on that land and the books
inside those buildings burned. It's said that it was
too hot, that the air changed, that people changed,
that commerce became not an idea but a beast
whose belly we live inside. All these intestines. Our
ancestors built glass over glass over glass and some
things were preserved, but most things weren't, and
some things died out, and some warm places that
made us feel safe were not. It's said the world ended.
It said the world died, that the sky was poisoned,
that we hid inside a capsule. It's said that magic
creatures are always at the edge of our world, trying
to reclaim it, but capitalism keeps them at bay. It's
said our cultures changed. It's said some cultures
assimilated into each other, some stayed intact. It's
said there were countries hours and hours apart, but
suddenly the earth was different, trips that would

have taken days took minutes. Countries that were never beside each other suddenly were. There were portals. Allurement. Devilry. Enchantments. It's said there were monsters. It's said that we were the monsters. It's said some people went on quests and saved the world, whatever that means. It's said the mall is our panic room. It's said the mall is our death chamber. It's said the mall is our world. It's said the mall is our salvation. Some people say that we need to protect our mall territories, think of humans first. But the mall is alive and it's always shifting and changing. If we give up, everything will change.

I won't give up. As long as I work at my tuxedo shop, everything will stay the same. Right? My job is my constant. My parents are my constant. My boyfriend is my constant. We will make our relationship work. We'll find a way to leave together. *How could I ever leave alone?* Even when I think these thoughts, I don't quite believe them. Even when I think of animals and monsters and magic, how I'm supposed to be skeptical, I don't quite despise them. The more I think I've learned, the more I realize I probably don't know anything at all.

When I'm walking back to clock back in, a rogue funnel plant—growing out of a planter in front of a Kay Jewelers—pops its mouthy lid at me as I pass. "Jwarrrshuaaa."

"That's not my name," I pause, spinning on my heel to face it.

"Carwashua...Goulashua..."

"Leave me alone."

"Saltmarshua. Jarrrshua. I have a prize for you, Jarshraaa."

"Everyone has a prize for me."

"*Joshua who has a good, kind heart*," the funnel plant whispers in a voice I don't recognize, yet that sounds familiar.

I creep over, tip-toe as all the people pass me. At the bottom of the funnel plant, in a pool of water, I see a beautiful bracelet, linked like dragon scales. Citrine lines its edges and catches in the light. It would look perfect on Banana's wrist. Maybe he'd reconsider staying at his job, moving in with me? I run my fingers along the carnivorous plant's lip.

"Yes, Jarshwua, yes. I have a favor to ask of you. Put your arm inside me. Just take the bracelet into your palm, and we will get to work."

Work! I recoil. I don't even look back as I hop from one teal tile to the next on my way back to the store. I recite old rhymes about broken mothers' backs in my head, pretend every other color is lava, that one misstep will result in the foot sinking, catching aflame.

When I return to the store the floor is strangely empty, but there are odd objects all huddled together in the center. A clockwork mannequin. A helium tank. Lots of half-rotted boxes. Silverfish swirl out from cardboard holes; I dash behind the counter to get my favorite dustpan.

"Remember that big shipment?" Stud smiles, stepping out from behind the mannequin like a cartoon villain.

"The one coming tomorrow?" I ask as the thousands of whisker-legs swarm beneath my broom. I make bolt to dump them in one of the planters in the median of our mall lane, where they will be safer and less likely to be stepped on.

"THE ONE COMING TONIGHT!" Stud yells at me through his cupped hands. Strangers passing by pause and turn to stare at him before moving about at their regular pace.

"And—there's a wedding party that called while you were at lunch. They're coming first thing tomorrow."

"So we need to have everything unpacked tonight," I say, and Stud repeats the same line back, confirmation in his voice overriding the inquiry in mine.

"Don't worry," Minaudière says, carrying the boombox out of the back, a crackling rendition of Ravel's *Boléro* trailing with her. "Stud, schlep that old junk to the dumpster so we can have enough room to inventory all the new rentals and tchotchke in the back."

I touch the half-rusted polish of the helium tank. "Do we have *balloons?*" I ask, as Mina laughs.

"No, tank's empty, but I found this." She hands me a spool of ribbon—like a citrine bracelet gilded in plastic—there must be hundreds and hundreds of feet wrapped around it.

"Can I keep this?" I didn't know I wanted plastic ribbon, the kind you tie to balloons, but for some reason it reminds me of Banana, and with that I feel a slight surge of euphoria moving through me.

"Sure," she says, and I slip it into the deep pockets of my work jacket.

I help Mina carry out mysterious junk from our storage space. A supersized bottle of aftershave as big as a helium tank. *Another* actual helium tank. Corsets all the color of slime. Suspenders patterned with human tongues. Gloves with a round hole in the palms—"So you could be formal and still get your palms read," Mina says, and I'm not sure if she's serious—lots and lots of zoot suit chains made out of hard candy. We carry them halfway to the floor, where Stud meets us and brings to the dumpster.

When we are done Mina and I sit in the backroom on a break, drinking water in a glass full of crushed ice, which is Mina's favorite kind of ice, and thus my favorite kind of ice. We, of course, are not supposed to sit, but because Mina is the manager, we sit.

"How is Banana?"

"Good," I say, "I love Banana," I say.

"I know you do," Mina says, and touches her gold and black nails against my knee. I notice a gilded ring inset with pearls around her left ring finger. Has she always had that? Am I noticing it now for the first time? We are quiet for a minute as her hand lingers. Mina pushes forward. I nod. "No one marries their high school sweetheart," she adds, before I even begin to tell her anything. Maybe this has been on my face for weeks? Maybe she knew it before I knew it? I suddenly feel both so visible and equally transparent.

"I've heard that, but why can't we be different?"

I say back, all the same. Even as the words come out of my mouth, they feel like a failure. They don't even feel like my words, they feel like words from a book, a billboard, words uttered millions of times before. I think of myself as the child I am, like I should be asking Mina about herself, her life, her ring, but the attention is always on me.

I'm not sure if I'm going to cry again, so I crush the tiny fragments of ice into my half-emerged wisdom teeth.

"You're taking a gap year," Mina says, "Joshua, I took a gap decade—no—a gap life." She cracks up at her own joke. "You'll have your big adventure one day." My head is bent low, focusing on the temperature of the cup as my hands surround, but when I gaze up to nod, I make a careful glance at the corner of Mina's eyes, looking for crow's feet, for the real age behind that youthful skin.

"Banana was supposed to work at his family's Dick's Sporting Goods, but he chose the kitchenware store instead. I thought this was the first step to us leaving our families. I thought maybe we could get away, move to somewhere like New Mall City. I thought we could live together, sleep in the same bed. I think he's going to go back and work for his family, and I am going to leave, and we are going to break up, or maybe we just did break up," I say all in a breath.

Mina strokes my knee. "Sorry that all I can offer you is a cliché, but growing up is hard. Don't misinterpret what I'm about to say, because it's okay to feel all of these things, but you do not have to feel all these things right now. The day is almost over, but we still have important work to do."

"I just want to go home and sit on the couch eating Dad's leftovers," I sigh.

"Don't talk about leaving yet," Mina says, taking her hand off my knee. "Don't rush anything. We got to talk about you becoming third key, anyway."

"What's that?"

"An upgrade," she smiles. "It means it's your job to open and close the store when the store manager and assistant manager are not present," she says in this mock-official tone.

"Are you and Stud going somewhere?" I ask. Mina pauses, looking me over. I look at her ring. She seems me looking at her ring.

"We both have to clock out early tonight.

I go to ask *why*, but I don't.

Mina once told me she got a tarot card reading done in a mall alley just a few streets over from our store. She said the psychic told her she would marry Stud. Mina said there's nothing wrong in believing your destined for something, as long as you don't presume what you're destined for. Once, Mina fell off a ladder while carrying some jackets to our highest rack in the back—the one where you can almost touch the dome glass beneath our green sky. I had never heard a scream like that. Stud and I were both out front. I saw that look on his face. It was the face of someone who feared he lost something that he couldn't get back. After he ran to the back, I followed, slowly hiding in a row of jackets. I was panicking. I didn't know what to do. I watched how his hand put ice in a disposable foot sock, held it there on her ankle. I saw him kiss her knee, which is when I stopped watching. There was something to this gesture, something I felt so outside of. Who was he? When they whispered I couldn't tell which voice was his, which voice was hers. I saw a Stud that I've never seen that day, and sometimes when I can't stand his sneering face I think back to that moment, try to imagine what *really* knowing that Stud would be like.

The deliverywoman comes; she is muscular, reminding me of the dental hygienist I saw this morning. She glides effortlessly, moving box after box into the center of our store. The deliverywoman makes small talk to Mina about some Neiman Marcus that closed down and became infested with talking rabbits and how she hopes our portion of the mall keeps business up. As the deliverywoman goes back to her electric palanquin to receive more boxes, Mina starts firing off tasks at me.

Mina is purposeful in her instructions of how to count the cash, where to put the receipts, how sometimes you need to tug at the front gate a few times on the left side before it gets loose and comes down. I know all of these things already, but I nod tacitly.

"Remember not to use the inventory code on the tag, but the one that's already in the computer," she says. Retail is its own world with bizarre, shifting rules. "And while overtime is not a problem, you need to be quick," she instructs. "I saw one of them cauldron dingoes drinking out of a fountain last week on my walk home late at night."

"There's no dingoes in this part of the mall," Stud says. "She's just pulling your leg."

"Better hope not, with how much of a baby you are, they gonna eat you first," Mina fires back. Stud looks half-wounded, but Mina winks at him and pats his shoulder. Stud smiles over my head at Mina, when he thinks I'm not looking. They're usually not this playful in front of me. For a moment, I see the two of them through a different vantage point and wonder how much of their bickering is insincere, just for show.

"Sign here," the deliverywoman says.

"JOSHUA JINNOUCHI, THIRD KEY," I write. The title isn't required, but I want to see it, want to put it down somewhere to make it real. Mina and the deliverywoman tsk-tsk a bit more about dingoes and crones and giant cats before the woman is on her way again in that beige uniform.

When Mina hands me the bronze key we use to lock the front gate, I feel a gush of adultness within. It has an ornate antique swirl at its bow, arabesque that curves down the shank toward the collar and throating of the key. There is a bowtie shape in the negative space of the bit. I love it, but I also feel a tinge of emptiness inside, like something sad has been passed off in my hands—as if I always expected Mina and Stud would be here forever—but what if they both quit before me?

Mina repeats the same instructions again and

again as she leaves. For fifteen quiet minutes, it's just Stud and me. I can't tell if I'm imagining it, but he seems calmer, more tender. He doesn't glare at me or order me around. He just stands at the cash register, staring out at the mall, daydreaming with a soft smile. When it comes time for him to leave work too, he puts his hand on my shoulder, and I flinch, imagining him grabbing the back of my neck. Instead, he gives it a light squeeze, a nice squeeze. When I go to look at him, it's not a smile, but it's not a frown either.

"You'll do great," he says.

I tell myself something Dad told me before, even though it's hard to live by: just because someone is rude, doesn't mean you have to dislike them. Just because someone is callous, doesn't mean you can't see past the hardened skin, to what is underneath. I think of Stud pouring that ice from a lunch soda cup into that foot sock, resting it against Mina's skin. There is something on my face too: neither a smile nor a frown.

* * *

I flip through Minaudière's old cassettes, pick one labeled in Russian, the boxy letters reminding me of monuments, temples. The classical orchestra that bellows out is both supersensuous and opulent. As if by possession, my arm moves to cut open all the cardboard boxes in rhythm, *shlick*, *shlick*, the box cutter sliding through the tape as cymbals crash.

It takes hours. Even after I lock the front

door, count the cash register, there are hours and hours of work. I burn through cassette tape after cassette tape. Even with the process figured out, all the pocket watches, herringbone waistcoats, hand-dyed ascots, and crocodile cummerbunds take hours to put in the computer, to find their proper home in the back. The final box—quite small—contains half-a-dozen bracelets, rubbery #2 pencils curled to make a perfect circle. I slip one into my pocket—for Banana—pull crumpled dollar bills from my other pockets. I set them beside the cash register, remind myself to process the order in the morning.

When I finally go to close the gate, I stand on my tippy toes and lift my legs off the ground. The left side is stuck. I wiggle. Eventually, it comes down. I wrap the chain around, fit the brass key into its home and leave this day behind me. I have never felt this tired, although I'm certain I've thought *I have never felt this tired* before. I feel my exhaustion ping through me in a hallucinatory loop.

It's after midnight, and nothing close-by is open. The teal avenue I work off is lit only by the gas lamps that limn. Everything else is the sweet lack that Monday nights bring. As I walk, I hear the heel of my boot clack against the tile and echo. I make myself walk softer, suddenly nervous from Mina's stories, of the deliverywoman's *tsks*, from that separation of safety—or an idea of safety—that daylight and crowds offer. Have I ever been this alone, out this late by the tuxedo shop deep in the country?

I live only a mile away from the store. It's about a good twenty-minute walk, maybe sixty seconds shaved off if I beeline through the Victrola Crown Food Court, which I do. The drunks passed out at tables with their margaritas in front of Chipotle provide me comfort. There are even mall cleaners and mall police in the area, standing by, doing their night work. I think about asking one of the policewomen to escort me home, but then I feel so silly. Am I not an adult? I move on.

Soon again, I'm alone, the hollow eyes of the American Girl dolls watching; the Brooks Brothers and Buckle and Burberry provide no comfort. Although I was alone in the store for hours handling merch, I now feel so terrifyingly unaccompanied. With all these stores closed, with the business in lull, the mall feels wilder, more frightening.

I try to think of what tobacco looks like, then I think of that hare, then farms, then my farm, then tobacco again, then Mina screwing around in a dead mall, but I don't want to think about Mina's naked body, so I think about dead malls in general, and then I think about nightdogs, and then I feel even more terrified. My hand brushes the pencil bracelet in my pocket. Fingering it, I realize: this fear isn't just from being currently alone, but of perpetually being alone. I am scared of losing Banana, scared of leaving this job, scared of having to figure out what is next in my life—realizing I've emerged on some other side past the automations that high school required. I've never even ridden in a plane. My entire life has been spent walking the same corridors of this mall—these same blocks—one after another after another. There is no one left to give me instructions, tell me how to become the person I want to become. I have to figure this mall life out for myself.

As I round another corner, there are small crowds of people again. This is a high-end street, one with a bunch of new businesses: two art galleries, a French fusion restaurant, a Korean barbecue spot. As I walk past the gogigui grill, something familiar flickers in my periphery. Through the dark glass at the restaurant's front, I see a dozen people dining together. The beer bottles and plates spread across the table like a miniature city. They are laughing, carrying on, all the banchan spread out before them. The closest to me: those two familiar faces. Mina is bringing chopsticks to Stud's lips. He grabs onto the jeon with his teeth, smiles back. It feels like someone poured a pitcher of iced water into my stomach. It's one thing to suspect something, to know it inside, but to be a voyeur, to peer through the looking glass into another world—to see it clearly—it reminds me of that day I hid in those jackets after Mina fell. When they kiss, this time on the lips, I turn, begin a trot that turns into a run.

My immediate thought is to run to Banana's place, but all those confused feelings fly around my brain—the worry of having to see his sick father. Would he even want me there? Was he not trying to break up with me? Are we even still together?

I think about how late it is. Who would welcome me? Where should I go? I don't want to go home, don't want to see my lonely father, be trapped in my lonesome bedroom where the desolation of our household would only become magnified. Besides my father and my overseas mother, are my two coworkers and my boyfriend the only people in my life? My aloneness feels three-dimensional, layered, sinking lower and lower into my feet. What about all my friends from high school I never talk to anymore? My old teachers? Has by past been swallowed by my part-time job, this dream of a constant future? Jogging still, I cut around bends, return to the dark avenues of the mall, away from whatever celebration I just saw.

Knowing Stud and Mina, what they hide away from me, I recognize some part of me, not quite adult. That was the other part of me I saw: my youth, my ignorance. Perhaps this part of me that is fearful, walking fast with my head down, so nervous that a plastic Pluto startles me as I turn the corner past a Disney store—perhaps this is the part that I will have to abandon. I will show them that I can go beyond this young version of me, this teenager. I can enter that adult world too. I know that I could still live everywhere like Mina lived everywhere. I could meet someone new, get married. Maybe I'll open up my own store, rent out my own tuxedos. There's a vigor in me, a "me against the mall" ball of warm red mist swirling inside: this internal fight of me against everyone who ever thought they knew me.

Halfway through my walk home is Labyrinth Aquatic Square. It is called that because the gorgeous fountain in the middle is a low labyrinth you can look down on. Most people don't know the difference between a labyrinth and a maze, but that's one lesson I paid attention to in school. The former has a singular path—one entrance that doubles as its exit—the task is to go to the center and to return. Labyrinths are disappointing because you always end up where you started.

This fountain is large and takes up most of the square, which is half-under-construction. It's been half-under-construction since I was in elementary school. The chain-link fence, plywood, and tarp cover half the fountain so you can only walk around one side of it. The other half-circle of the fountain goes down some abandoned corridor to a dead JCPenney, and no one goes down dead mall pathways at night, unless they are brave, horny, stupid, or all three.

Above the fountain are Edison light bulbs popping with disco lights. I usually stop here, both walking to and from work—although I've never been here this late before. Opposite from the fountain is a row of banks, and all the bankers are gone, probably in bed, like I should be. It's surreal and calming to see the lights like this when the green sky has disappeared: bright lights and their reflections dazzling through and across the fountain water. It's so stark against the dark surroundings. The pink fading into yellow fading into green fading into blue: it's like a nightclub without the music, a nightclub after all the humans have been raptured away or gone home. I'm so pulled into these illuminations that by the time I snap out of it, I realize my heartbeat has slowed, that there's almost a comfort in being here alone.

It's feels like this square has its own kind of

temperature, except it's not felt on the skin; I feel it somewhere inside my chest, my throat, my head. It feels similar to when I'm offered quests, some dizziness inside my brain. Is this magic? How could a place with so many banks fill me up with sensations of sorcery?

I sit on the tile side of one curve of the fountain, take the pencil bracelet out of my pocket, hold it up to the disco lights. If there is spellwork here, in the air, then let it fix me and my life. I want to look at this bracelet again, to see this thing I got for Banana, as if looking through the center could create a portal that would let me look straight to his face, let me see him and our love clearly. I squint, trying to count how many sides the pencil bracelet has. I twist it clumsily in my fingers. Six? When it slips, I say "*Shit*," quietly, but it feels like a possibility. It feels like something I knew could happen in the uncharted depths of my mind. Every action resulting in a change, in the world unhinging slightly. This is what magic does: it moves through you like sequence, like divination. Half of me feels like crying at losing the bracelet after working such a long day, but I refuse myself. I know who I have to become.

I watch the bracelet go around all the bends— tight waterways of the fountain like the pink curves from an anatomical drawing of the human brain. Where the rusted fence and moldy-rot plywood dips down in the water, the bracelet slips under, to the other, unseen side. Dark side, uninhabited side. Abandoned JCPenney side. I walk around and wait, squint my eyes again, as it's harder to see in these discotheque lights—but the longer I wait—the more I know the bracelet isn't emerging from the dead mall side of the fountain, the fence.

I climb. Of course I climb. I slip my finger in the diamond slats of the fence and rise. Halfway up, between a tile wall and the outer-most side of the fence, I find a spot where the metal curls, where the wood is gone, and slip through, balancing on the top, staring toward the dead mall side.

There is no light, or, little light, but I feel the deadness filling the air like smoke. There are only the remnants of the pink and blue and green and yellow popping from the active side where all the banks are asleep. I stare into total darkness, the total quietude of the dead mall, and I descend the fence to retrieve the bracelet I got for Banana.

I feel the *what-are-you-doing* beat coursing through me like the water from the fountain's bends. I've been to pop-up haunted mansions around Halloween in this part of the mall, where things are more decrepit. My heart feels that memory, entering that lightless space, like a teen in a moon ghoul costume might pop out and scream into my face at any moment. From this spot, I can see the neon popping back in shattered glass across the tile floor, colored reflections in windows with the pale, empty faces of mannequins staring at nothing. In middle school, once or twice, I hopped the fences and walked toward dead mall areas with my friends, but it was always during the day, where we could see the green sky through the glass ceiling, and we were always chicken and ran away after barely a minute.

Now, in this older body, I carefully descend into the darkness, letting my foot fall on the thin tile edge of the fountain's hidden side. I squat. After my eyes have time to adjust to the obscurity, I can see the thin strands of disco light sneaking through to this dead side—above and below—and see the gentle splash of water running its course. And then, a few feet away, there it is, caught on some curved hook of fence dangling down in the water—the rubber bracelet! The yellow paint on it is caught in a beam of light so it nearly glows. It wiggles and bobs as the novelty bauble it is. I don't even ask myself about my need for it. I only feel a heated clot of meat throbbing somewhere between my throat and my chest: some anxious organ I do not have a name for telling me to *go, go, go.*

When my arm swings down to grab it, so does my foot stretch to a new place on the tile fountain's edge, a new place inhabited by fresh, uncracked glass, now cracked. The newly ground shards create a dim echo through the tiled chamber I awkwardly crouch in. When I look nervously into the black space, searching for anything that could be listening, four gilded eyes reflected by disco lights return to meet mine. It is one of those possibilities, those instincts: always looking for an enemy in the darkness, but never believing you'll actually find one. The chilled water on my fingertips enters me, my whole body becoming a tundra inside.

"Child," she says, in a voice husky and ancient. I think of crystal caverns, although I've never seen one. I think of fog billowing past quartz. A chemical smokescreen moving across an ocean, although I've never seen one of those either. The remnants of the rainbow lights' reflections move from the other side, leaving the phrase *aurora borealis* in my head. Whose memories are these? What's happening to my thoughts? I stand to meet the spell inside the voice. I look up at the fence in front of me, slip the pencil bracelet from my wet hand to my dry wrist. "You're thinking of running. I'm faster," the voice says. "You must come closer, let me have a good look. You can trust me."

I do as I am told. As I come closer, walking across the edge of the fountain as if it were a balance beam, I see who she is, why she's the only one talking. Leaned against the wall on the opposite side of the sealed-off territory I entered, is a hare, propped up with its chest excavated, as if for surgery. Its dead eyes disco ball in the ghost lights. Beside it, a cat, as big and dark as a panther, but with a face strangely domestic, licks her paw.

"All alone," she says. "Let me see your hands." Her crescent moon eyes refract. I hold both palms out as she instructs; she paws at the bracelet. I feel hot, sticky blood gel against me. Her paw as big as— bigger than—my own, the claws lightly rub down my palm, as if reading some aspect of my past, although she certainly must know about my present and future too. I only look at my hands, then, slightly, to the hare.

"You're not a nightdog," I say.

"Much worse," she says. "Those dogs don't go

anywhere near me." She chuckles. "They can become shadow, but I *am* shadow." The pointed tip of her claw draws invisible symbols in my hand. "Ah," she says, her pinpoint claw stops on a line I don't have the name for. "Joshua..." she says. "Joshua, who is destined for greatness..." "Joshua..." she says a third time.

I nod at her in the veiled darkness.

It's strange, how this is not much different from the entities who visit me when I'm working the store during the day. Mostly, I'm alone there too. But something feels different, beyond the shift in the florescent light of the store to near-total darkness. I feel as helpless as the dead hare spread out before me. Is this what magic means? Was everything I'd been told about these creatures true?

"I need you to do me a favor," the cat says. "I am gathering for my children. I am bringing back dinner. We have settled because we cannot move. One of my children cannot move. One of my children is stuck. For days I have brought him back dinner, Joshua, for he is stuck in a place I cannot get him out of. I've dropped the meat down to him, but I fear he isn't eating. I need assistance. I need your thin, human hands, Joshua. I need you to save my child."

I look at my hands. I've never once considered them *thin* or *human*, but regardless, they are. I nod at the darkness, again. It's a nod like: yes, you are a cat who is talking to me about your children and I am acknowledging that this is my current reality.

"No," she says, "I need you to agree out loud. I need us to make a verbal pact. There will be rewards, but I do not want you to do this for rewards. You need to do this for Joshua." There is a sincerity to the she-cat's tone, and I'd never want a baby to starve because I refused to help. Is she telling the truth? Of all the offers I've passed up, is this the one I'll say yes to? I'm frightened, and I'm in a dead mall, and it's late at night, and shouldn't I be home eating leftovers? Shouldn't this all not be happening?

What will you do if I decline?" I say, hesitant.

"Think of this as a quest, Joshua. You always have the option to decline—but I want you to think of my poor, trapped cub. I think this is an important chance meeting, Joshua. It is a chance you, of course, can walk away from."

"They say if you go on a quest you become less human, that that mall swallows you whole."

"*Humans would say that*," the cat whispers back. "They're very biased. I could tell you another story from a much different perspective." I can hear a small smile in her tone. "It's a long story, about what happened to this world—but you must do me this favor first."

I stare through the dim fragments of light at the hare's body for what feels like a long time. "I will help you," I say, thinking of that word, *reward*, thinking of that word, *quest*, thinking what they could mean, what everything I've been told about the world I live in could mean.

"Carry that hare with your strongest arm," she says. "I need my mouth to talk to you." I swoop the corpse under my right armpit, hold it close to me like baby doll. Its fading warmth, its smell. "And your

other hand, grab my tail. There is darkness ahead
of us."

We walk down the center of the mall avenue
in quiet. We move away from the glow of Labyrinth
Aquatic Square, toward a dead JCPenney that no
one goes to—at least—no one human inhabits. My
eyes keep trying to adjust but they don't. I look up,
knowing there are glass domes above me that give
the eye access to the sky, but it must be a starless
night, because every direction I look is near-pitch.

At a certain point I am only my ears and touch,
only the dead hare hugged into me, its warmth
fading and fading, only the soft bristle of the tail
touching my palm. Occasionally the cat speaks,
"Joshua, who has a good heart, a good, sad heart."
or "Joshua, who was born on a farm." I don't have
the knowledge that this cat has. I can't say anything
back about her. I may not have any extra-sensory
powers, but I have a warm bed, a job, and I don't
live in some lightless wreckage down a foreclosed
mall alley. At the same time, what am I even doing?
Why am I trying to feel smug and superior to this
palm-reading cat who could snap my head off with
one bite? I know nothing of this cat beyond what
she's told me. Why say *yes*, why now? Is it because
of that poor baby? Is it because I wanted to prove
myself to people who don't even know I am gone?
When I imagine her kittens in my head, they are
hardly small and pathetic. I can't imagine something
of her size ever being smaller than a football helmet.

"*Where is your child stuck?*" I whisper.

"You'll see," she says.
"I can't see," I say.
"You'll see," she says.

When we get to the JCPenney, it's by her instruction alone I know we're there. The entire front glass is boarded up. I rub my right hand against plywood briefly. I'm too afraid to let go of the tail. Even as she instructs me to duck down, to crawl through a hole, with the dead lagomorph dragged under me, I don't let go of her tail. It is my one safety, my one promise against all the other imagined jaws in the dark rushing toward me. These childhood fears of darkness course through me, and this cat is my nightlight.

When we emerge on the other side there is a red emergency light hovering above us like a maraschino cherry, like a hat, like some murderous disco—powered by electricity unknown to me. She wasn't wrong: I do see. It's as if everything is coated in a thin film of cough syrup. I wait for moon ghouls to descend, for some blood-banshee to scream and chomp down on my throat, but there is only quiet.

There are old metal hangers, racks, mannequins—fallen over, upright—they all stand like ancient torture devices in this sinister light. Even though I can see, I don't let go of the tail. I've gone into a world that few humans ever enter, which is strange, thinking about how it's only a few blocks from the fountain I—and hundreds of other people—pass daily.

"Where are your babies?" I ask her.

"I have a temporary nest—at the other side of the department store. We must save my lost cub first."

"Where is the cub?"

"Down there," she says, pulling me along. We approach an old escalator, destroyed by who knows what; perhaps blaming *time* is enough. Some of the metallic stair steps are missing, destroyed, bent. There is a crevice beneath the strawberry light. I see robotic guts, gears, all the ruin of this machinery as it descends down into some darkened basement level of the store. I've ridden up and down an escalator before. I've never considered going *beneath* one, *inside* its core.

"My child has fallen down there," the mother says. "I am too big to fit down there. Leave the hare here. Climb down. You will find him at the bottom. You will bring him up to me."

I think of what Banana would say. Or Mina, what advice she could give. This is far different than fucking in an empty fountain *near* a dead mall. I have entered one, I am inside it. I can feel its magic in the air, nearly oppressive against my skin. It's almost like a parasite inside of me now.

I think of Mina's shamisen music, how staticky it sounds, crisp out of the old mini-boom. Although it was my music first. My mother's. My father's. I have to stop thinking of myself as a shell of a person. I have to become whole. Here, there is no familiar music. Here, there is only silence, a filament of the red bulb buzzing on, maybe, if I listen hard enough. There are options, of course, but there is also the

one thing I can do: go onward. I look down into
the belly of the escalator, its dark core, far beyond
the light which bathes the open store space like
nebuchadnezzar after nebuchadnezzar of wine. I
inch closer and closer.

"Yes," the cat says, "That's it." I let go of her
tail, feel the bracelet spin, and my hands now open,
pressing against the cool air.

Although this department store must have
been uninhabited for ages, the old gears my hands
push against feel like they are newly wet with grease.
I could just be imagining this. I've never had to
depend on the sense of touch so intensely before.
Everything is fingers, is the deep breath exiting my
mouth and how aware I am of both these parts
being so, so human. Into the belly of the escalator
I crawl. There are sharp metal parts and soft metal
parts and rubbery belts and I have to be careful as
I descend down. It's clear, immediately, that some
space beneath the escalator has rotted away—that
I'm now inside some wall? Floor? Some part of dirt
falls away as I grab into what I thought was more
wall. I'm now part of some deep stomach with wires
and plaster and grease on all sides. If the mall is
alive, I've lowered myself into the bowels of its deep,
ancient body.

"Hello?" I say. "Baby kitten?"

There is no response. Inside the body of the
mall is a hum, then a slither. A stench of rotten meat
rises to greet me. There is a dread in the bottom of
my gut, but there is something deeper, some belief
toward something superior, something new I don't

quite have the knowledge of yet. A continuation. A better *after*. Like that temperature inside my, for lack of better word, *spirit*, I feel something warm and hopeful despite everything around me being ghastly. I've gone this far refusing to imagine my death, and I will not do it now.

From somewhere below me I hear a sad mew. I rush. I know I should be careful, but I want out of this mechanical void as soon as possible. A slither; another slither. I climb down clumsily, letting my foot rest on whatever gear or belt or metal part it can touch. I cut my hand in the darkness. I can feel the red of the blood rising to my skin, but I can't see it. I try to lower myself, to meet more metal, but my hand touches the surprise of cold dirt and mud.

Something below me groans. It is not beastly, but earthly, like tectonic plates readjusting. It moans and hisses. I reach my hand into my pocket, feel the yellowness of the balloon ribbon, but cannot see it either. There are no more places for my foot to rest. I keep stretching one foot down, then the other, with nothing to land on.

Then, I feel it, the weight of something small. I almost recoil, leap back up toward the red light, but I realize these claws are baby claws. The crawl. The tiny pin-prick claws dig into my socks. The baby cat mews again, ascending me.

"Hold on," I say, "We're going back to your mama." In automated gesture I grip the interior of the escalator with one hand, throw the spool around me with the other. Just like fitting a customer for a tuxedo. I spin the spool around me again and again like measuring tape, tie the kitten neatly to my chest. "I hope this doesn't hurt," I say, feeling the little warm body strapped to me. "We will be back to your mother soon." Something below me groans again, but with a growl, growing louder, coming up higher from the dark depths of whatever I am inside. I cannot see colors or perceive space or know how deep whatever below me descends, but there is something down there, and it is coming. With my two hands free, I scramble up. Every grip I make is hard and certain. I would slam my fist into the edges of a knife if it gave me the grip to climb higher. I do not look down, I do not mis-step. I climb and climb. I climb toward my life, toward that cardinal light drenching everything in red.

* * *

When I crawl out of the hole I run and duck behind the giant cat, looking back at the metallic wound. "There was something down there," I say.

"It was only my child down there," the mother cat says, although she sounds a bit hesitant. I'm not sure why, but I think of that hesitance as human, and like an onion one small layer of the cat's mystique feels peeled back. She feels, even in one small portion, slightly more knowable.

She extends her long, bladed claws and rubs them closely against the balloon string tying her child to me. It unravels. The purr of the mother is deep and comes from the heart. Reunited, she cleans the grease off her child with her tongue, scolds the cub in a language only known between the two of them. It's a harsh mother tongue, and I can understand why the baby only responds in mews. After she is done, after the child has been cleansed, she brushes against me, although she is tall—the side of her body brushing against my upper chest. I still have one eye on the hole, although no other sound has been made. Wherever I stand, I make sure the giant cat is positioned between me and whatever was in that dark belly.

"Thank you, Joshua," the cat says. "I saw in your lines that you could return my child."

"Can you see my future?" I ask, mind half-elsewhere.

"I can see *futures*. Nothing is predetermined. I saw that you were terrified of me, but that you were scared of living your old life more—and beneath that—a sadness in you that I would never see my child again. You didn't accept my quest because I intimated you—you accepted it because you understand what it could mean to lose someone. Joshua, who has a good, kind heart."

Her kitten pounces at my feet, begins to crawl up my pant leg again, its own baby-needles sinking into my skin, reminding me of all those afternoons I sewed buttons, accidentally pricked myself in the thumb. I help the kitten up to my shoulder, where it rests.

"What do I do now?" I ask, although I know this cat doesn't know. I just want someone to answer it for me.

"You should at least sleep in my nest where

I can watch over you tonight. Everything is safer when the green sky returns. I could walk you back to where we met in the morning, if that's what you want. There are options, though."

With that, she grabs the bloodied hare into her mouth, moves past all the empty racks, shimmering. I follow her deeper into the store, farther away from the mall life I came from. Although she doesn't tell me to, and although I can see, I hold her tail. It gives me the strength to look forward, to not look back at whatever I left behind, at whatever could still be following.

In the farthest corner away from the entrance, there is an old dressing area. In the farthest end of the dressing area, there is an unusually spacious room—tattered maxidresses and board shorts and bras line the floor. In the bed of scrap fabric, the kitten hops off my shoulder, joining its two—three—six siblings. They all mew excitedly at the returned one—noticeably the runt—all the fluff-balls chirping in their cat-language.

Although hungry, I pass up on the invitation for raw rabbit, letting the children dine. It's quiet for a long time as the young teeth gnaw. The kittens look less adorable with blood smeared on their mouths. Lying back, letting my heart still: I'm aware of how my eyes have adjusted to the bloodshot light in all this darkness. I think about how bizarre this is in comparison to being third key.

"I have to be at work tomorrow," I talk to the dressing room like I talk to the empty store.

"Is that what you want to do?" the she-cat replies back.

"I don't know. I want *something*—and even if that *something* is different from what I have now—I can't just completely walk away. I'd have to at least quit my job before I figure out what that is. I'd have to see my parents again—even if I'm trying to get as far away from them and my life as possible. I'd have to officially break up with my boyfriend. I can't just not see everyone I know ever again; they'll think I'm dead—and anyway—it's not like I can live in a dead mall's department store. Frankly, I'm not sure how you're living here," I say as I look down at the hare's bones scattered on decrepit panties. I feel all these thoughts spilling out of me into the redness.

The she-cat moves closer, pawing at my hand again. The kittens draw closer to me.

"There's other options, Joshua. Remember the reward." She walks to the other corner of the dressing room, picks something up in her mouth, drops it at my feet.

At first, I think it's a tooth from an extinct creature called a shark—I have a similar tooth I keep in a shoebox under my bed. Instead, I realize it's a claw.

"It snapped almost entirely off when trying to fetch my child a few days ago. I tore it off when I got back. I knew I kept it for a reason. There is power in my body, Joshua. I need you to empty your pockets. Take off that bracelet too."

Although I don't fully understand, I do as I'm told: my house keys, my wallet, the bronze store

key, the balloon ribbon, my phone, the bracelet for
Banana.

"I came here to hunt, Joshua. I came because
a smell brought me through a milky door. It's an old
door, it's not like your doors. It's part of a pathway
few humans know how to use. It's a door I came
through, perhaps, to meet you."

"I thought you said nothing is predetermined."

"All I know is that tomorrow I will leave
through that same door with my children. Know this:
you can come through the door too. This is a deal
I am making, an arrangement, which starts now: if
you hold that old key, you will be instantly brought
back to your place of work. Your house keys: your
home. That bracelet? Your love. If you hold my claw
between your fingers, and think about a different
world, you can come with us. Not forever, but for
awhile. This is your reward, though: permission. A
motive. Recognition that you can leave, that you will
survive for a little longer. That you can leave your
loved ones. That you will see them again, although
it will not be for a long time, and you will have
changed, be unable to look at them the same after
you have left them. This is the magic I have granted
you, and thus it is so."

"And what happens if I go back to my old
life?"

"That's up to you. You can continue your
life. You can work your job. See your people again
and again. Your kin have taught you to be afraid—
rightfully so—but there's wonder in the territories
you deem *dead*. There's are reasons beings like me

offer you bargains, deals, quests, and not all of them are as malicious as you've been told. You don't have to decide tonight. This day was long, and the night continues. It's not the bed you're used to, but these old garments should be soft. Whatever you decide, I'm grateful." The she-cat leans in, her heavy head brushed into me, pushing me back into the clothes. "You're a child too, Joshua, but you exist in a moment of your life where nothing is not possibility. That's why magic loves you, humans your age like you. Magic seeks transformation."

When I close my eyes, I can still see some soft pinkness through my lids, feel the baby fur of the kittens walking around me, brushing up, climbing over my chest. All my senses have become queer and distorted, and the pictures in my head seem somehow real, sharpened, as if my eyes weren't closed at all. Whenever the she-cat speaks, it feels like some strange magic physically enters the air from her throat, lingers after, even into the quiet. It feels like it moves into my lungs and blood, throughout my body. I recall stories from my childhood, myths, anecdotes passed down through generations from my parents to me, other experiences from my own life. They all seem so intertwined, so vivid as I pass off into sleep.

* * *

I dream of Banana and me on a beach, at the edge of a large ocean. The ocean isn't like the ones inside the malls that have another mall on the other side. This ocean is boundless. There is no glass dome surrounding it. You could sail indefinitely. The sky is sky, and that sky is blue as the ocean we stand in front of. It's all like the old movies I have back at home filmed in the before. Banana is helping me push a giant bento box toward the water from the shore. Each compartment has supplies we need to go about our new lives. When we push the bento boat onto the surface of the water. It floats. I hop in, laughing. I'm sitting up front, paddling. Banana is supposed to be sitting behind me. I speak to Banana about our adventure, about how everything is different now. When I turn to see my boyfriend, he's not there. I'm already one hundred, two hundred feet away into the water, but I can seem him clearly—he's on the shore, waving. He's smiling, but also, he isn't. I look into the bento boat, and there's a hole, a leak where water is shooting up, as if out of a whale's spout. Something taps the side of the boat. It's a raft: one made of giant cowboy killers tied together. I climb overboard, fall flat onto the raft. The paper wrapped around the tobacco is dry. Even though we're in the water, the cigarette raft begins to become lit at one end. I don't know where the fire came from, but it makes the raft begin to diminish. I'm moving farther into the distance as the raft both shrinks and sails. I keep trying to turn around to look back at Banana, but all my movement is strange, and the entire world is covered in a thin layer of smoke.

* * *

In another dream, I'm on my childhood farm, at the edge of the crops, pressing my fingers into tempered glass—the wall at the edge of the farm that separates it from other stores of the mall. Looking over my shoulder, I see Dad with a hoe, breaking up the soil. I'm sure the vegetables at my feet are tobacco plants, although they look like bok choy. My body becomes ghost, becomes jelly, and slips through. On the other side of the glass I enter a pre-mall world, an ancient Japan where I see my great-great-great-great-great-great-great-great-great-great-great grandmother playing the shamisen. Beside my ancestors, my mom sits seiza-style, with a ceramic mug in her lap. She smiles at me. There are dancers moving all around her in beautiful, over-designed clothes. A drama rolls out across the wooden floors as actresses pop out of thin area, delivering playful, rowdy, bawdy, hilarious lines. Feeling a tap at my shoulder, I turn, and see Mina smiling down at me. Behind her, holding her hand, is Stud. He is smiling too. He is different from the Stud I work with. He might be a Stud that only Mina can know, although I see him clearly now, in the pathways of this dream. I feel a tenderness for him, a forgiveness inside me. I know this is a dream because of how unfamiliar this Stud feels, but as soon as I remember the dream, that I'm dreaming, the thing itself blurs, and I forget I'm asleep, I lose my lucidity, I'm pulled beneath the enchantment of the slumber.

The light and the landscape of the dream

changes, but Mina and Stud are still with me. They motion me to follow them into another room, which is the backroom of the store we work in, although all the clothes are gone. It's just skeletal rack after skeletal rack glimmering in a red light. The rows seem to stretch out toward infinity. Mina, taking the lead, opens the door to the smoking closet, pulling Stud in behind her. I follow.

Not a tiny closet, but huge! We are in some box seats, looking down at the Victrola Crown Food Court—except it isn't the food court—it's only a model of the food court. It's like a theatrical arena! All the round seats are full of fox spirits and hares and crones and mummies and kobolds and gryphons. Bunraku puppets dance around below, on the center stage, carrying little wooden trays with artificial soda bottles. We watch the puppet show from above. A puppet version of Banana and myself are moving to our favorite booth. All the puppet-people around puppet-us are chanting, the chords of the shamisen plucking louder and louder, carried from one dream to the next. It's almost like my eye is a telescope, and I can look down, seeing the cartoon cat pattern across the vinyl seat the puppets sit on, bursting from flat design into the third dimension. The she-cat's kittens are floating out of the fabric like balloons. They are real kittens, but they are also full of helium. A yellow balloon string is tied to each of their tails, and as they pass me, I grab on. I try to grab Puppet Banana, but he withdraws his hand, smiling at me again.

The smile says: it's OK. The smile says:

forgiveness. The smile says: go.

The kitten-balloons are taking me far away. I pass the box seats, and Mina and Stud wave at me too. They are no longer human versions of themselves, but puppets too, and their big bubbly eyes smile as they wave and wave and wave. I ascend into the green sky, where a tornado spins me higher and higher, where the sun is a red sphere that never stops buzzing.

* * *

In my final dream, I wake up in the middle of the night in the dressing room. With my eyes closed, my sense of touch returns first—all the warm bodies and fluff of the kittens snuggled up against me. Although I'm groggy, I see an unfamiliar figure in the doorway when I look around. Although I've never seen one before, I know it's a nightdog. Its pitchy fur almost sucks the crimson light from around us. Its long, pointed devil ears rise up toward the ceiling. The light blurs into a blackness as it slithers forward. Its eyes are a kind of purple-turning-blue, like the disco lights from the closed-down fountain that spun me to this world just hours before.

In my dream I see its long nightdog teeth, but they look more like human fingers than teeth. Long, white fingers hang out of its nightdog mouth, each fingernail sharpened to a point, wiggling at each joint. Its sharp, wormy teeth curl and uncurl in its mouth as it approaches me. I feel for the kittens sleeping against me, trying to push them farther into my body, hidden under my arms. The nightdog's head dips low, its teeth-fingers flex down to meet my fingers from the hand that shakes. There is a groan, a hiss, a moan—not from the nightdog's mouth, but from deep within its core.

From behind me: like someone turned a cooling fan switches on. A dark breeze. There is only a low growl, then there is the she-cat grabbing the nightdog by the throat, dragging it away down the dim hallway, away from her babies, away from me. My heart should be beating in some fear-burst, but the body is so tired in this dream, the little bodies of the babies so warm, and so...

* * *

The morning light seems so pure coming through the glass domes that fill the abandoned department store's vaulted ceilings. All my dread from the night before has left, hidden away with the emergency lights that shine true only during their own terrible night hours, but now that redness is entirely drowned out by the sun. Everything is white-ish, is blue-ish, is a cool, powdery green. The she-cat is stretched on the floor. Her babies are spread out before her, fighting to grab on, nurse.

"Did you sleep well?" she asks me.

"I didn't sleep *unwell*," I answer. "I felt like I had these vivid, swirling dreams all night, but I can't remember them. They felt *good* though, like, I can feel the feeling of them. It's like when you solve a really difficult math problem."

"I don't know anything about that," the she-cat purrs, "But I do know the mind is always working, even when we sleep. Sometimes it takes us places, crosses great psychic distances, to give a solution."

"Were they even....?"

The she-cat smiles, then looks down at her children. "They're getting too old for this, but still they need to grow. They may look like the cats you are familiar with, but they will never stop growing. They will become my size. I will keep growing too. They need good bones, Joshua. I need good bones too. They need to know how to hunt. If you join us, I will teach you too."

"I don't know if I am the hunting type. Do I have to tell you my decision now?" I am on my knees, gathering all my ordinary talismans to shove them back into my pockets.

"No, but soon."

"I would like to see your magic door." I smile.

The she-cat eyes me. "When we reach the door, you only need to touch the object that fulfills your desire, the one that will return to—or take you to—wherever it is you are going."

After the kittens eat again, they are quiet and stumble behind their mother as we walk opposite the way I entered. There are glass cases that I can only imagine once contained perfume and make-up when this department store was inhabited, was kept alive by the moving bodies of humans and all the dollar bills that passed between their hands. The counters are shattered now, broken down into remnants. This entire store that shook me just hours before looks so benign in this dull light.

I second-guess the night before, wonder how I could have ever been scared. It makes me feel sad and wistful more than anything else. We pass a plastic, bald mannequin head on the ground, and one of the kittens pounces it as if it were a soccer ball, or else, prey. Their mother gives a hearty laugh. This, too, makes her feel more familiar, human, like someone I've known for a very long time.

At the end of our path is a set of doors, but where the glass should be, there is only a strange, milky gelatin. The door looks slightly out of place, like some prop from a New Mall City musical. It looks like one giant semi-translucent marshmallow is stuck in the wall.

"It's safe to touch that?" I say, holding my hand up.

"Don't—not yet, Joshua. Let us walk through first. You'll be able to pass. Still, there is a lot you do not know about this world yet."

"And you're going to be the one to show it to me?"

"Only a fragment. I promised you my story. If you accompany us for a while, you will have it. Whatever you do, there will be fragments."

"And all I have to do is touch the object that will take me wherever I want to be?"

"And think about it, really think about it. It's magic, but it's not complicated," the she-cat laughs again. There is a joy coming from her throat, a renewed life inside her. "These old pathways will understand. They're the avenues that reconstructed this world. They're the avenues that we've always walked down, so do not be afraid. Whatever you decide—thank you, Joshua."

Now that is it lit inside by the sky passing through the glass domes above, I realize I can look—I mean really look—at the she-cat. I can see her dark grey coat, the hints of blue in the fur, and the coolness, and the warm gilded depth of her eyes. She keeps reminding me of someone, but maybe that's just the charm, the sorcery of whatever corner of this world she came from. She turns, brushing hard against my clavicle as she moves past, into the thick wall of white confiture. All seven of the kittens look at me with some type of appraising gaze, some look I don't quite understand, then follow their mother's footsteps. I go to reach out, to call her back. I wanted to tell her about my dreams, or else *ask* her about them. But maybe she already gave me those things I needed: the permission, the motive, the reward. Forgiveness.

Mina and Stud would be okay without me. Banana would be okay without me. My parents would be okay without me. I could teleport back to my bedroom, hug my father. I could go back to that store with my third key, make it my own. I could move out of my parents' space with this new energy, withdraw all my savings from the bank and go to New Mall City with only the cash stuffed into my socks, my bag.

And then, too, there's this other world, the one I thought I always knew. My little corner of the mall always felt small, but now it feels smaller: atoms, crumbs, ash from the mysterious cigarettes locked inside the smoking closet's walls. In this other world, is there anyone who could love me in the way I desperately want to be loved?

When I close my eyes, I can almost teleport my emotions to the previous night, how scared I was in the belly of that lightless escalator. Those fears are gone. Plunging my hands in my jacket pockets, I touch all the objects, their textures feel heightened, synesthetic to my fingers. The bronze key like an escalator's gear, the glass screen of my phone like the curved surface of a bottle of wine. Sweetness. Nebuchadnezzars. Objects resembling objects. How the corner of the she-cat's claw cuts into my fingertip, accidentally. I feel a drop of blood rising again. Taking my hand out of my pocket, I hold my fingers, what they grip, up to the daylight. The red of me looks so stark against the facet of the smooth nail. I rub it one more time, feeling its texture, its familiarity, as if it came from me, was always part of my skin.

Fordite Pendant

Ambien, Benadryl, melatonin: nothing works. Some part of me resists, lying in bed, eyes screen-bound, body pulled between unconsciousness and the rubber buttons of the remote. Their toyish texture under my thumb. The blue of the TV magnifying out of its box, voices of the dead echoing from another room.

Hallucinations are a known side effect of resisting such sedatives. The brain is made up of so many chemicals—but isn't everything made up of chemicals? In the bedroom, in the TV, half the channels are dead, and the cartoons that play are never the right ones. Too much Felix, an excess of Popeye. I hunger for Monument Valley: Wile E. Coyote painting those elaborate extensions of the desert right on the side of a rock. Deep sediment. A trick of the eye. The joke would go like this: the Road Runner doesn't know it's a mural, so he runs right through it, speeding into a fake horizon. When Wile E. tries, he smacks into hard rock. *Trompe-l'ohwell*. I always wondered where that place was the Road Runner went to. It was just an illusion, but that false landscape went on for miles. Those cacti weren't real. That sun wasn't real. Yet, he went there. Maybe none of this matters, but these are the thoughts that get me through five-thousand A.M., slipping past my own calendared murals and one notch closer toward sleep. My mind winds down from the frantic, remembers a childhood in front of a similar screen, watching the same shows. When I fall sleep—if it's even sleep—my mind plays a re-run that goes:

A father has five sons and four of them don't love him. They have their reasons. They say he was a hardened man—cruel. By the time the youngest arrives, there is a gap, an asymmetry. The four sons are old enough to be the fifth son's father, but they are not. The father is older and softer. He has retired. The four sons grew up in Detroit. Now they live everywhere. The fifth son grows up in Ft. Lauderdale, where his mother calls him *the white sheep of the family*, where the father takes him fishing every other weekend. He is just a little boy, and there is a little boy seat in the back of the old, sturdy bicycle. His father tells him this bicycle is the last American bicycle. That all the American manufacturers are defunct, just part of the great decline in what was a good industry. The father teaches his son the importance of fish, the importance of kindness, the importance of bicycles, and the importance of cars. The importance of being industrious. The boy is older when the father has a heart attack while driving the old pickup. The boy is the passenger. He has to see the sparks of the metal truck against metal railing before he grabs the wheel, realizes how real this reality is. How the impact in the ditch could in some way be described as delicate, although it wasn't. How he tears at a packet of Bayer that the father kept in his glove compartment. First with his teeth against plastic, then his fingers pushing against the father's tongue, just trying to get the antidote somewhere into the body. At least what I thought was the antidote—I mean—what the boy thought.

Maybe it's not a dream, these things that happened. My brothers were too involved in their new families, their ham radios, their coin collecting, their legal jobs, their paid vacations, their honeymoons, their online classes, their motorcycle repairs, their marriage counseling, their Scuba training, their gambling, their *Calvin and Hobbes* mural paintings in the nursery. Three of my brothers showed up for the funeral. One didn't. I tried my hardest. I stayed up night after night trying to write a speech. At the ceremony my boisterous mother told everyone to be quiet, when everyone was already quiet. She announced she had to have a few last words with her man. Even my seasoned brothers chuckled at her spirit. She didn't cry. When it was time to give my speech, I wept only three words into the delivery. *My father was...*

The past tense is always the most damaging. In my sleep I am always alone. I kept the American bicycle for too long. It rusted at its edges. I named it *Happy Birthday Grandpa* and shortened it to *H.B. Gramps*. Why did I call it that? Was the bike that old? Did everything feel old? Was the country I lived in old? I thought this name was clever, thought it made me feel younger, although I already was the youngest one. I went to a bike skill-share group where I learned hub from rim. The previous occult mechanics of the bike split itself into human anatomy. Everything had an organ, a name. First, Gramps was de-rusted, fixed—outfitted—but then I moved on to building other unnamed bicycles from scratch. I gained the ability to build a road bike with my eyes closed. I learned how to paint them, the perfect gloss of ultramarine. I replaced Gramps.

Then came the races, the cross-country journeys with only the sun crackling my pink shoulders. I'd stay in motel beds. I'd watch cartoons. Even with how exhausted the body became from these long treks, the sleep never came easy. My endurance only grew. I resisted that other journey into my nights. I had these moments where I saw strange faces in the stock art on the motel walls, or else heard the voices of my brothers coming from the bathroom. Time was a dream too, how it made me foolish.

Sleep paralysis: I couldn't move my body, but I felt my dead father sitting at the edge of the bed. I couldn't turn my neck to see him, but I remembered his weight, the feeling of him visiting me early in the mornings to announce some catchphrase, some cereal prize of wisdom. He told me I needed to go to *the old home, the home from before I was born*. He told me I needed to see where he worked, to understand what it meant to be American. I went alone, on my bicycle, all the way back to Detroit, where I had never been. I stood in the painting bay of the old Ford factory for hours, marveling. It was long enough that someone noticed. A tour guide approached me.

My father worked here, I said. He had the largest hands I have ever seen, I said. The great decline of the American industry, I said. The beauty of automotive enamel, I said. The beauty of cobalt like contusion, I said. He loved all five of his sons, I said. I've tried to do it too, I said, as a hobby, I said, and on bicycles. I tried to love America—and industry too. I don't know what it means to be American, I said. America is a flower coming to bruise, I said. I am not my father, I said. I tried to stay awake, I said. It's not the same, I said. There's so much failure. I said I miss him.

Let me show you the ovens, the tour guide said. If your father worked here, you should see this. How they baked the car frames to cure the paint. How hundreds of layers of paint—all colors—dripped into the walls as psychedelia. One paint dried atop another, hiding its beneath: all that chromaticity. How later, people noticed, salvaged the slag from the ovens' interiors. How it was beautiful and otherworldly and resembled agate. Agate is a stone, he said. Patterns like prismatic lava. You should take this, the tour guide said, handing me a small cube of the Detroit agate.

I biked for a long time with that "stone" tied to the front of my bicycle. The dissected colors as a beacon. I went home. I took a job at an art studio in Ft. Lauderdale where I assisted a local painter in creating murals for corporations. I later quit that job and became an auto detailer. My brothers criticized me, said I was becoming my father, although which aspect could they mean? I took a knife to the Detroit agate, carved it down into a teardrop shape. The layers of hardened paint resembled a crystal, something worth millions, although it wasn't. I had gotten the largest portion in the will. I had burned through the money. I quit my job and donated plasma, did sleep studies for extra cash. I wore the pendant wherever I went: a clasp, the enamel almost holding a glow of its own, lightly tapped my heart.

I sleep with it always. In testing chambers, with the EKG wires worming all over my body. The cold gel, the stickers, the air-conditioned room. My brain. The voices of my brothers visit me as hypnagogic ghosts, although they continue to live. They whisper about the falseness of fathers, of America, of industries. Something about silence, about cruelty. The falseness of this stone wrapped around my neck. How could a few decades compare to millions of years? The stone is still young and worthless, although what is anything in this world worth? Who can put a value on a bicycle, on a stone, on a father?

At night, in bed, when I finally give in, I can hear the ACME sound effects. The cannons. The TNT. The coyote's body smashing against rock. *Meep-meep*. A choir made entirely out of my father's voice, calling me down, telling me to bring my fishing rod, that these are the worms that the grouper like best. The sheet beneath me is lowering in intervals: first fast, the pendant bouncing up, then tapping me on my chest, slow. Its dried layers of paint make an empty thump. The center of the bed is a funnel that I descend through. The sheet is rock and that rock is just lithospheric layers laced with color: mandarin orange, champagne, deep cherry, black, forest green…. All the gorgeous shimmer of cars is there, in the core of the earth that calls me down into its hot interior. I think of all the imperfections, here, and then, too, a future in which all these blemishes could even be cured.

Acknowledgments

Earlier versions of these stories appeared in *The Account, Barely South Review, Cicada, Hotel Amerika, Mississippi Review, Ninth Letter, Sonora Review, Tampa Review*, and *Wyvern Lit*. Thank you to all editors and readers at these various literary journals who believed in these fictions and gave their time and energy to help them become something.

To my family for always being proud and supportive of my creative undertakings, even when they didn't make sense.

To Michael Martone, who guided me with kindness and encouragement and pushed me to keep going, even when I was out of breath. To Julia Coursey, Reem Abu-Baker, and the rest of my fiction MFA cohort (as well as the faculty) at the University of Alabama.

To Dawn Raffel, Tim Jones-Yelvington, Sam Cohen, M. Milks, Nicole Treska, Joshua Boardman, Leah Schnelbach, Micheal Hooker, and all my scattershot fiction friends.

To all my friends and literary comrades in New York, that place where I was learned.

To the following residencies and workshops, who graciously gifted me time and space to work on this manuscript: to the spirit of Edna and all the kind folks at the Millay Colony; to Margot Farrington and Tony Martin for their urban bird nest; to the

Edward Albee Foundation for their barn at the end of the world; to the kind and thoughtful staff at the Key West Literary Seminar; to Lambda Literary and my dearest Golden Step Square Pillowfortians.

To Lidia Yuknavitch, who saw these misfit words as possibilities. To everyone at Lake Forest College who had a part in this process—and Madeleine P. Plonsker, to whom this book would not exist without her patronage and generosity.

To the hundred or so poet friends who are unnamed here—thank you for giving me a language and a sense of self. I imagine quite a few of you will find yourselves named in the Acknowledgments section of *Mask for Mask*.

And last, but certainly not least: to Faust, tuxedoed muse and impish familiar of endless adoration and charm.

Biography

JD Scott is the author of the poetry collection, *Mask for Mask* (New Rivers Press, 2021). Scott's writing has appeared in *Best American Experimental Writing, Best New Poets, Denver Quarterly, Prairie Schooner, Indiana Review*, and elsewhere. *Moonflower, Nightshade, All the Hours of the Day* is Scott's debut story collection.

The Plonsker Series

Each year Lake Forest College Press / &NOW Books awards the Madeleine P. Plonsker Emerging Writers Residency Prize to a poet or fiction writer under the age of forty who has yet to publish a first book. The winning writer receives $10,000, three weeks in residency on the campus of Lake Forest College, and publication of his or her book by Lake Forest College Press / &NOW Books, with distribution by Northwestern University Press.

Past winners:

- Meg Whiteford, *Callbacks* (fiction)
- Jessica Savitz, *Hunting Is Painting* (poetry)
- Gretchen Henderson, *Galerie de Difformité* (fiction)
- Jose Perez Beduya, *Throng* (poetry)
- Elizabeth Gentry, *Housebound* (fiction)
- Cecilia K. Corrigan, *Titanic* (poetry)
- Matthew Nye, *Pike and Bloom* (fiction)
- Christopher Rey Pérez, *gauguin's notebook* (poetry)

For more information about the Plonsker Prize and how to apply, visit lakeforest.edu/plonksker

For Mom, Dad,
and Jonas